NIGHT
OF
MYSTERY

BY **MILENA**

1. INT. SPACESHIP MANNA-373 – ACADEMY ON BOARD, LECTURE ROOM – DAY

Miss Marry is giving a lesson to 12 young cadets. They are dressed in MANNA-373 uniforms with a geometric sunflower logo.

MISS MARRY

There comes a time when even galaxies cannot stand alone, because their own power is insufficient for protecting them from outside dangers. COOPERATION across the universe is necessary for the well-being of all.

CADET 1

Does that mean there is only friendship in our universe?

MISS MARRY

I can say that COLLABORATION prevails, despite all differences between the subjects.

CADET 1

How are those differences handled?

MISS MARRY

Very simply – by the Universal Laws. These Laws bring order, yet allow for temporary and local disagreements, separations and even wars. Our spaceship, Manna-373, pays special attention to areas populated with entities of dualistic consciousness, who still live through conflicts and sufferings. Rough circumstances they generate stimulate the fastest learning within the Dimension of Evolution. No experience is evolutionarily useless.

CADET 2

Dimension of Evolution – could you please elaborate, Miss Marry?

MISS MARRY

It is a vast domain of space-time matrix, where evolution through a specific energy range is lived. The objective is to experience duality and transcend it, by reaching unity consciousness. The Dimension of Evolution has its own laws and ordinances, which, of course, comply with the Universal Laws.

She looks around as if to tell them she reads their thoughts.

MISS MARRY (CONT'D)

Before you enquire more on the Universal Laws: they are electro-magnetic fields, energy fabrics which organise everything – from physical formations to administrative and mental levels. This vastness within the Dimension of Evolution, that we are gliding through, is therefore a neatly organized medium. For its wellbeing, high consciousness is a must. Why high consciousness? What do you think?

CADET 3

Only high consciousness can recognize the necessity of order and willingly support it.

CADET 4

Such consciousness understands ONENESS and interconnectedness, which means: if I hurt myself, I hurt all others.

Satisfied with the participation of her students, Miss Marry glances over the entire audience.

MISS MARRY

Excellent! Always keep in mind the Oneness of the entirety of Creation – it will best direct your actions. With this, let us conclude today's session. Thanks for your time and attention. And, of course, it is your turn now.

All cadets visibly change focus towards their inner selves; stand up and, with their right hands over their heart areas, utter in a soft yet well-projected voice:

12 CADETS

(All together)

I am a being of light and love. With mighty power inside me I can discover my essence-self and serve the universes. I am grateful. I am honoured.

The lesson is over.

The cadets slowly get up, move around, chat with one another and start leaving the lecture room.

Cadet, ITA, a young blond female with extra short hair, approaches Miss Marry. We do not hear their conversation.

FARO, a young crew member, appears at the door of the lecture theatre and looks for Miss Marry.

She notices him, and nods her head to acknowledge his presence.

As Miss Marry ends her conversation with Ita, they walk together towards the door and meet Faro there.

MISS MARRY

Hi, Faro! Let me introduce Ita to you!

FARO

Nice to meet you, Ita.

ITA

Thank you, Faro. Nice to meet you too.

FARO

I hope Miss Marry has not overloaded you with information today?

ITA

No, not at all. I am like a sponge – there is always a space for new knowledge.

FARO

> Then, Manna-373 and Miss Marry
> are ideal teachers for you.

They smile.

MISS MARRY

> Ita will finish her training soon and
> be ready for an apprenticeship
> placement. Do you know of any
> position where she could join?

FARO

> As a matter of fact, I do.

2.   INT. / EXT. MANNA-373 – SPACE

*From the lecture theatre, a rapid zoom out all the way
to the outside of the spaceship MANNA-373.*

*For an instant, we see the geometric sunflower logo on
its outer shell.*

*Manna-373 suddenly speeds up and merges with the
distant interstellar mist.*

3.   INT. CAMBRIDGE, BALLROOM – SATURDAY
EVENING

*An elegant banqueting venue hosting the dinner party
apropos the graduation anniversary of MBA students.*

*Jolly atmosphere. Old pals are relaxed; chatting,
laughing, drinking, dancing. We follow PAUL, LIAM,
NORA, BRUNO. CHEN, DANIEL, GLEN, AABI and RON.*

DANIEL

I cannot believe 20 years have passed
from our graduation! So many things
have happened since... It seems as
we live in a different world now.

Daniel turns to Chen.

DANIEL (CONT'D)

How are things in China?

CHEN

China has always had its own way,
which the West either cannot or does
not want to understand. Despite
being burdened with such a big
population, China is doing well.

AABI

If you asked about Nigeria, I could say
the same.

BRUNO

In Brazil, it seems as THE WAY IT IS –
is meant to last forever and nobody
will notice.

PAUL

Unless, perhaps, a great global
challenge forces us to change and
evolve faster as a civilization?

NORA

A civilization!? What makes you think
that humanity on Earth has become a
civilization?

PAUL

Are we not a civilization?

NORA

A civilization recognises and applies
the same values and laws in a
uniform manner across the whole
planet: as in Papua New Guinea so in
the US. Clearly, we are not there yet.

PAUL

I see. That is one way to look at it.

LIAM

Instead of pondering into serious
matters, I have a better idea. Nora,
can I invite you to dance?

*Nora gracefully stretches her hand to Liam and
addresses the rest of the group:*

NORA

Excuse us.

*Liam and Nora leave and move towards the dance
floor. Others continue their conversation.*

BRUNO

It is interesting that you, Paul,
mentioned a global challenge as a
catalyst for a faster evolution. The
change I am dreaming about is the
switching from consumerism to a
more humane and creative format
of society. However, changes can be
of a different kind and, talking about

them, I cannot help but remember
the information a Brazilian shaman
gave me recently. He talked about
a mysterious cosmic influence that
will hugely disbalance the population
across the planet. He also mentioned
problems with memory.

CHEN

No, do not say that, Bruno!

Everyone looks at Chen.

CHEN (CONT'D)

A few days ago, I had a dream with
identical content.

*Suddenly, all seated around the table exchange the
glances of wonder.*

After a while, Aabi breaks the silence.

AABI

If you are still thinking that it was a
coincidence, just one of many that
happen all the time, and before you
dismiss it, I also feel summoned up
to share with you my most peculiar
recent experience.

GLEN

Must be a good one, since you are
making such an introduction.

*Glen is alerting everyone with his glance cruising from
face to face.*

GLEN (CONT'D)

We are all ears.

AABI

I was sitting by my laptop, writing
a covering letter for one of my
business reports. At one point, I
noticed that my fingers carried on
typing while my mind was empty.
I felt absent from that action yet
one with it. There was a lightness in
my entire being – no pressure, no
discomfort; but not even thoughts
were there – only awareness of the
process. I do not know for how long
that state lasted. When the report
was finished, I read it and found a
section utterly unrelated to what I
intended to write. Definitely, that
section did not come from me, even
though my hands wrote it. I do not
know how it happened, who dictated
the sentences, how I was taken
under control, and many other things
related to it I still cannot explain.

RON

YES, I did not expect anything less
from you!

*Some laugh, while the faces of the others reflect the
speechless state of their mind.*

GLEN

And, what was delivered through
you? What's the message?

AABI

Exactly the same as what was told
to Bruno and Chen. I would have
perhaps dismissed it, if I did not
hear the messages they received.
Now, when I consider that the
same message came through three
different ways at three different
locations on the world and to friends
who were to meet soon – I have to
take it seriously. I do not know about
you, guys, but I believe in Holy Trinity
and, consequently, do not take lightly
anything that comes in threes.

4.   INT. CAMBRIDGE, BALLROOM – SATURDAY
      EVENING (CONTINUED)

Dance floor.

LIAM

So nice to see you after many years.
You look great!

NORA

Thanks. You have not changed much.

After a while.

LIAM

It was interesting how you described
a civilization. I always adored your
unique perspective. However, I never
dared to communicate that fondness.

I was afraid, actually – not sure how I
would handle your reaction.

Silence.

                    NORA

Perhaps, it's my turn to be sincere.

                    LIAM

Why not?

                    NORA

Would you believe me if I tell you
that I also admired so many things
in you and, perhaps, most of all a
kind of mystery that was enveloping
you. You were there yet remote, as if
belonging to somewhere else. There
was always an unbridgeable distance
between you and others – at least
from my perspective.

                    LIAM

Did you admire other guys for their
uniqueness as well?

                    NORA

No, I did not.

                    LIAM

Have you ever thought of building a
bridge between us?

                    NORA

Of course, I have... but I never dared
to start.

Liam stopped dancing and looked straight into Nora's eyes. She accepted his gaze with no resistance.

> LIAM

May I ask why?

> NORA

You seemed utterly uninterested in me.

5.   EXT. CAMBRIDGE, GOLF COURSE – NEXT DAY, SUNDAY MORNING

Early morning, abundant in sunshine.

Daniel and ERIC, early 50s, childhood best friends, are equally enjoying their golf session and the company of each other.

> DANIEL

Long-time since I've seen you. Does it mean MI5 cannot do without you?

> ERIC

Far from it. I can easily be replaced... my mother was rather well lately, so I was not visiting her that often.

> DANIEL

Does she still make that fabulous rhubarb crumble?

ERIC

Oh, yes! She does. You could pop in and I'll ask her to make it. She would love to see you.

DANIEL

Let's do it next time. This time, I prefer you to come to my place to meet my MBA pals. We celebrated our 20th graduation anniversary last night, and they are still here. I expect them tonight for a dinner with my family. They have something very interesting to share, and I would love you to hear it.

ERIC

You are a master in creating irrefutable invitations. See, now, you've given me unexpected homework. I have to come up with a good excuse for my mom, for not playing cards with her tonight.

DANIEL

Then, suggest playing a matinee session instead.

6. INT. CAMBRIDGE, DANIEL'S HOUSE – THE SAME DAY, SUNDAY EVENING

Daniel's house is a typical higher middle class English cottage with a spacious well-maintained garden.

His family is a happy lot: wife ROBERTA and three kids: TINA (19), MARTIN (13) and NICOLAS (7). All are seated around a dining table, together with Eric and the three esteemed MBA friends (Aabi, Bruno and Chen).

As they finish the main course, Martin and Nicolas get up to help Roberta remove surplus dishes and set up the table for the next course.

From the kitchen, Roberta is bringing out an apple crumble dish, followed by Nicolas holding a jar with custard sauce.

After the crumble was served to everybody.

DANIEL

I think it will be great if you tell us,
what you shared last night, about
enigmatic messages you picked up
recently. Martin and Nicolas, perhaps
you could greet our guests and take
the crumble into your room.

With visible relief on their faces, the boys cheerfully do as suggested.

MARTIN

Dad often mentions the time when
you studied together. It was nice
meeting you.

NICOLAS

Have a good evening.

We see the boys heading towards their room with plates in their hands.

At the same time, we hear a motorbike horn.

All are alerted.

> TINA
>
> I am afraid I will also have to leave you now.

> ROBERTA
>
> You have not yet finished your crumble?

> TINA
>
> True. Sorry, mum. I am processing the messages our guests were sharing. What unusual revelations!

After offering her big smile to everybody.

> TINA (CONT'D)
>
> It was a pleasure meeting you all.
> Enjoy the rest of your time in the UK.

She waves to her parents and joyfully leaves.

7.   EXT. CAMBRIDGE, THE STREET-SIDE OF DANIEL'S HOUSE – SUNDAY NIGHT (CONTINUED)

Tina runs out of her father's house to kiss her boyfriend, MAX.

She joins him by taking a seat on his small rather shabby Vespa motorbike. They drive away.

Max is a peculiar combination of a modern tech young man, motorbike lover, and an expert in esoteric knowledge. His dark, curly hair is never tidy.

8. INT. CAMBRIDGE, NIGHTCLUB – SUNDAY
   NIGHT (CONTINUED)

The scarcely lit dancefloor is packed with swaying bodies following the sounds of electronic music.

Max and Tina are dancing; she seems not fully present.

> MAX
>
> Is everything ok with you?

> TINA
>
> I suppose so.

> MAX
>
> Why is that?

> TINA
>
> I do not really know. Actually, I know – but would rather not know what I know now.

Having heard that, Max takes Tina's hand and leads her away from the dancing crowd.

They choose a quiet corner and sit comfortably there.

Max is posed to listen.

> TINA
>
> My dad had some friends at dinner tonight, and they shared some bizarrely acquired messages. Even though those messages sounded odd, I felt they actually announced a real scenario.

MAX

What scenario?

TINA

From what I gathered, some people
will have memory problems.

MAX

Sorry, but why do you think what you
heard was true?

TINA

As you know, I do not only rely on
words. I FEEL the energy as well.
… Yes, to me – it is true, and the
messages they received are a kind
warning from beyond our dimension.

MAX

Still, we cannot be sure?

TINA

Maybe some people can! But time
will tell. I personally do not need to
wait for any official confirmation.
I already have an urge to do
something about it immediately …
even if a tiny, tiny, step – it doesn't
matter… Just to initiate an action in
that direction. The rest will follow.

Long silence. They look into each other's eyes.

In a gentle gesture, Max embraces Tina's delicate
hands.

After a while:

MAX

I have an idea!

9.   EXT. CAMBRIDGE, OUTSIDE NIGHTCLUB –
     SUNDAY NIGHT (CONTINUED)

We see Tina and Max on the motorbike riding through the quiet streets.

The motorbike stops in front of a detached house.

Max pushes the motorbike into the gated front garden and leaves it there.

They enter his ground floor flat.

10. INT. CAMBRIDGE, MAX'S FLAT – SUNDAY
     NIGHT (CONTINUED)

Open plan moderate kitchen / dining area leads to a spacious lounge area oriented towards a modest garden.

TINA

You know, Max, I always feel good at your place.

MAX

Do you want me to be surprised?

Max walks towards his computer corner.

He switches the computer on.

Tina sits next to him.

MAX

> Let's see what our global community thinks!

He starts typing. We follow the words popping up on the computer screen:

- *"AVE, INMORTALIS, AVE!*
- *How old are your parents and how are they doing lately?*
- *Anything unusual to share?"*

Immediately, a stream of responses begins to flow on the computer screen.

- *"My mum is 45 and is getting significantly slower in thinking – the Moon could orbit around the Earth while she is choosing her words and pronouncing her sentences. This is a rather sudden development"*
- *"Good question... Mine are fine, but I notice my uncle's cognitive functions are rapidly deteriorating"*
- *"Dad, 55, occasionally struggles to remember what he has just said..."*
- *"Out of the blue, my older colleague (late 50s) is in a problematic situation... remembers just a part of our conversation... Her company does not know for how long they could count on him"*
- *"My father is only 49 and is really struggling to think and remember. I am worried."*

The camera distances from the screen where responses continue to appear.

Under the burden of these realisations, Tina and Max move their attention from the computer screen and spontaneously sink into a prolonged silence.

21

> MAX

So, IT IS REAL.

> TINA

Any information about it on the internet?

Both take their mobiles out and start searching.

11.　INT. / EXT. CAMBRIDGE, DANIEL'S HOUSE –
　　　THE SAME DAY, SUNDAY NIGHT

Daniel and Roberta are at their house entrance saying goodbye to their guests.

> DANIEL

Safe trip home – the best pals in the world!

From outside the house

> CHEN

Thanks for the great hospitality!

> AABI

God bless you and your family!

Bruno waves and sends his kiss.

At that moment, the house phone rings and Roberta hurries to answer.

Daniel is closing the door.

> ROBERTA

Dan, it is for you... your mother

DANIEL

(to his wife)

Thanks!

DANIEL (CONT'D)

Hello!

DANIEL'S MOTHER

Darling, I really apologise for calling
this late, but I need your help.

DANIEL

It is never too late, mother – I am
yours 24/7.

DANIEL'S MOTHER

I am getting worried about your
father. Recently, he has been
having some strange episodes. I
witnessed him literally being unable
to think. On top of that, he does not
remember those moments at all.
Actually, not only those moments but
many others. Not long ago, one of
his colleagues called me to express
his concern since Chris had those
episodes at work as well.

DANIEL

I see.

MOTHER

I took Chris to the GP and he
arranged for a hospital appointment
for further checking. That

appointment is tomorrow, but some unexpected things at work happened so I cannot leave earlier. I wonder whether you could accompany your father to that appointment?

DANIEL

Sure. Do not worry, mom. Leave it to me.

12. INT. CAMBRIDGE, HOSPITAL CORRIDOR – NEXT DAY, MONDAY DAYTIME

Daniel is sitting in the hospital corridor, waiting for his dad to complete the visit to the specialist doctor.

His phone rings.

DANIEL

Hello.

AABI

Hi, Aabi is here. Just want to thank you for a great time with you and your family last night. I am flying to Nigeria today... Look, I was thinking about the messages that Bruno, Chen and myself received. Perhaps, we could have a group chat about it in a day or two.

DANIEL

Good idea. Speak soon.

The female doctor opens the door and invites Daniel inside the room.

DOCTOR

Mr Dean, please! You can come in.

13.   INT. CAMBRIDGE HOSPITAL, SPECIALIST'S
      ROOM – MONDAY DAYTIME (CONTINUED)

Daniel's father, CHRIS DEAN, is sitting in a chair.

The Specialist Doctor walks to her chair and sits there.

DOCTOR

Have a seat, Mister Dean, shall I say –
Junior!?

Daniel takes a seat alongside his father.

DANIEL

Of course, you can. Thanks.

DOCTOR

(addressing Daniel)

All scans and other checks of your
father's health do not show any
abnormalities. We could not identify
any physiological reasons behind the
symptoms that he is experiencing.
We will see him in three months.
Anything else I could do for you
today?

CHRIS DEAN

Thank you. I will see you as
suggested.

DOCTOR

Certainly, Mister Dean.

Both men get up and a make move towards the exit.

Daniel opens the door.

DANIEL

Father, could you please wait for me
for a moment?

FATHER

Sure.

Chris Dean leaves the room.

DANIEL

Thank you, father.

*Daniel stays inside the room, standing, and addresses
the specialist doctor.*

DANIEL (CONT'D)

If possible, I would like to ask you
something not directly related to my
father?

DOCTOR

What is that, Mister Dean?

DANIEL

I hope it will not be against your
professional ethics to share general
observations.

DOCTOR

It will help me if you could be more
specific.

DANIEL

Recently, or relatively recently, have
you noticed any increase of this kind
of symptoms among your patients?
Or, an unusual increase in any
ailments?

DOCTOR

Yes, I have. But I am afraid, I am not
in a position to tell more.

DANIEL

I understand. However, is there any
way to give me a hint?

DOCTOR

Not more than directing you to the
latest scientific papers and reports of
health authorities. Good luck, Mister
Dean – Junior.

14.   EXT. CAMBRIDGE, RIVER CAM WALKING
      PATHWAY – DAY

*Daniel is by the river Cam, talking to his MBA pals via
group phone call.*

DANIEL

How are you doing over there?

CHEN

The sun is still rising in the east and setting at the west.

AABI

My dog is ill.

BRUNO

Sorry to hear that. I hope it will recover soon.

DANIEL

Guys, I am now fully convinced that your messages relate to OUR time on the planet. I have some supportive evidence.

CHEN

What evidence?

DANIEL

As it seems, my father is out of the blue having problems in thinking and memorising. I also did some research and found a scientific paper dated earlier this year, which had the following sentence: Compiled evidence suggests a high possibility of memory loss and impairment of thinking process in population over the age of 50. Further research is urgently needed. I am trying to contact any member of this research team.

By the way, are there cases of people's troubles with memory over there?

BRUNO

Brazilians are very social. Here news often spreads amongst people faster than through the main stream media. There is a rumour about suddenly impaired memory and thinking functions, even in people who are not too old – exactly what you described is going on with your father.

CHEN

During this short time since I returned from England, I have come across several such cases. But, not a single mention of this kind of problem in public media.

BRUNO

I am planning to visit a shaman, who hinted at this situation when I met him lasst time, to see whether he has some guidance.

AABI

I could also go to the traditional divination master to find out what the spirit world can tell.

CHEN

Then, I wonder how the Buddhist monk will elaborate on my dream.

DANIEL

Excellent! After I dig through the
scientific data, we might have a fuller
picture. Speak soon.

15.   EXT. CAMBRIDGE, DANIEL'S HOUSE GARDEN
      – DAY

*Daniel is sitting by his garden table, working on his
laptop.*

*He takes a break, takes out his mobile phone and dials
a number.*

*From a distance, we only see him talking and get into
his conversation after a while.*

SCIENTIST (V.O.)

Yes. We are conducting a wide study
that includes universities on all five
continents. As a matter of fact, that
study is in its concluding stages.
Results are being compiled now. We
will have the final report very soon.

DANIEL

Would you be so kind as to let me
know when the results become
publicly available?

SCIENTIST (V.O.)

Sure. It is actually in just a matter of
days.

DANIEL

Thank you very much indeed.

Immediately afterwards, Daniel dials another number and enters into a conversation.

DANIEL

Hi, Eric. How are you doing?

ERIC

Busy as usual.

DANIEL

Do you remember Garry, from Uni, the guy who used to look more to the sky than where he puts his feet on the ground?

ERIC

Mark! Yes, of course! I would sometimes play Chinese chess with him. He studied astrophysics, and later did his PhD in Oxford.

DANIEL

Do you still have his contact number?

ERIC

Most likely.

16. EXT. OXFORD, PUB – DAY

Eric and Mark are sitting in the outside area of the local pub.

Daniel brings three glasses of beer, and joins their table.

MARK

Good old Lager – drinking it with you
reminds me of the time when we
were students.

DANIEL

Mark, we have a specific reason for
this visit – besides, of course, to
enjoy your company and catch up
with you.

MARK

Whatever the reason is, it is great to
see you pals.

ERIC

Daniel and I are trying to understand
what is going on with our planet and
know not a better person then you
to find that out. Is there anything
extraordinary happening now in
relation to Earth and energy coming
from Space?

MARK

Hm, there are two answers to it.

DANIEL

What do you mean?

MARK

I mean literally – depending on
whom I speak to.

With my colleagues, we discuss
what we see on the celestial charts

and what we can tell from the data continuously harvested through our instruments.

According to relatively recent evidence, our planet and solar system have entered a magnetic field of alarmingly strong and unknown energy.

ERIC

How do you deal with that finding?

MARK

We have only detected that phenomenon, but cannot explain its origin or its full impact at the moment.

DANIEL

You've mentioned a second version of the answer!

MARK

Yes! The second answer is that we have identified a new cosmic cloud (Cloud-X) that has swallowed our solar system, but do not mention anything strange or alarming about it.

ERIC

Why do you have a double standard?

MARK

I would not call it a double standard
but our operational policy, meant to
protect the public from panic.

ERIC

Interesting! Who do you think you
serve with such work?

MARK

It is an approach that we believe
is correct. Why would we alarm
the population and push them into
fear, when we still cannot give an
explanation or help them with our
knowledge.

ERIC

Though I got your point, Mark, I am
not impressed with that attitude. To
me, it is more like a weakness of your
entire profession that is unwilling to
admit their own limitations publicly.
Excuse me, but I could even associate
it with arrogance: maintained on
the premise that the public does
not deserve access to all scientific
findings – basically to the truth. Such
a discriminative attitude could also
be seen as a manipulation of the
public, whom you are supposed to
serve most sincerely. Mark, sorry
for being so direct. This is just my
personal opinion and, of course, I
could be wrong. Actually, I wish I was
wrong.

MARK

Interesting perspective. Good to exchange stances. Daniel, what are your thoughts?

DANIEL

With the appearance of this cosmic cloud, the whole planet seems to already be affected and yet this is just the beginning. Medical evidence suggests that the thought mechanism of those over a certain age, which seem to be even 50, cannot incorporate the frequency range of the new energy on the planet. They cannot think clearly, cannot cognize and memorise their experiences – and all that without any tangible physiological cause. The truth, sitting behind the ramparts of the scientific citadel, does not really promise a lot. Sorry, Mark, the hidden truth is a wasted potential.

MARK

So, then, what do you think I should do, or we scientists should do, in view of this situation?

DANIEL

Science is hugely important for overall planetary progress, no doubt. Scientific research, and more so the management of scientific findings, determine our future. So, I think that scientist should stand in the front line, protecting the best interests of humanity, not only theoretically but practically – at least, by not hiding the truth.

MARK

You cannot say scientists are not working for the best interest of humanity!

DANIEL

You are right; and I am not implying so. I believe that what scientists are trying to achieve is exactly what all people are striving to do – and it is to understand life, reality, and ultimate truths. However, experimentally and repeatedly provable hypotheses are not the only indication of the truth – as scientific methodology suggests.

Daniel is refreshing his throat by taking a sip of beer.

DANIEL (CONT'D)

People, young and old, can conceive unique ideas and explanations of phenomena, outside the scientifically trained mind. I tend to believe that knowledge is the offering from the infinity of the Electro-Magnetic spectrum. As such, it is equally available to everyone – including scientists. To tap into it and bring it down, does not seem to depend on one's academic degree. How did Dogon people get knowledge about the Sirius star system?

MARK

Thanks pals – you have always been helpful. You made me think in a new way. Thanks for coming. Cheers!

Garry raises the glass of beer. Daniel and Mark follow, and they all toast to the moment.

17.   EXT. OXFORD COLLEGE COURTYARD – DAY

We see Mark walking through the College corridor.

He meets two of his colleagues (JONATHAN and MARCEL) who chat while heading in the opposite direction.

MARK

Are you joining us for the meeting at 5pm?

JONATHAN

I am planning to. How about you, Marcel?

MARCEL

Certainly. See you later.

18.   INT. OXFORD COLLEGE, MEETING ROOM – DAY (CONTINUED)

A small meeting room.

Mark with five of his Oxford colleagues, all astrophysicists, are seated around a centrally positioned table.

MARK

How do you, guys, feel about this
cosmic Cloud-X?

ED MORRISON

Aah, it is just one of many
phenomena we cannot explain.
There will be new ones for sure.

MARK

Would you think the same if you
knew that this interstellar cloud was
lethal?

MARCEL

What makes you say so?

MARK

Common sense. Since Cloud-X carries
stronger energy than ever before
detected in the vicinity of the planet,
it might have some undesired impact
on all life on it.

ED MORRISON

If we even knew its impacts, how
would that knowledge be relevant to
our astrophysics research?

MARK

It is ours to find out. Besides, I
believe that sharing the truth is
useful to all scientists and other
population segments. If we are aware
of a possible devastating impact

of Cloud-X, would we not try to do something to minimise or avoid it?

JONATHAN

We have already published our findings and made it available to everyone.

MARK

True, yet, this time, somehow, I feel it might not be enough.

MARCEL

You want us to step into the main stream media and alert the population of their POSSIBLE DEMISE? HOW WOULD THAT BE USEFUL?

ED MORRISON

Why would we change our operational protocols?

MARK

Because those are not written in stone – the same as scientific knowledge. As time goes by, new findings make some protocols and knowledge obsolete. Every moment, our universe, solar system and our planet encounters new energy on their cosmic journey – and that matters. Does it not?

ED MORRISON

Of course, of course... nobody
disputes that. But, I am curious to
understand whether you advocate
that we invite all people, all branches
of science, even artists, philosophers,
and spiritual community leaders to
a debate on the cosmic Cloud-X, and
do all that on the public platforms?

MARK

Something like that – why not?
Together, we could have a wider
insight and, in a way, will share
responsibility. Would you not feel
better in such a case?

JONATHAN

Suppose some crazy ideas are
conceived at such an open brain-
storming platform, would that
mean that we should listen to an
eccentric artist or a fanatic spiritual
figure about what humanity should
do? To accept their unscientific,
unsubstantiated ideas would be
equal to leading the entire civilization
to an abyss.

MARK

I would not go that far in
anticipation, but rather arrange our
appearance on certain mainstream
media and take it from there.

ED MORRISON

I am not convinced it is a good
idea. Actually, I am convinced it is a
dangerous one.

MARK

If something can be done, let's do
it. I'd rather actively seek a solution
than feel helpless.

JASON

I am still wondering what we are
going to do, when we actually do not
know what to do!

KEVIN

Wait a second guys, information
about the Cloud-X discovery is not
our personal possession. If it is to be
disclosed widely, we need to seek
permission from our department. Do
we not?

19.   INT. SPACECRAFT MANNA-373, FARO'S
WORKSTATION – DAYTIME

*Faro and Ita are seated at their joined semi-circular
desks, made of translucent material that shimmer
with internal glow.*

*There is no clatter on the surface; with very few buttons
or levers; no keyboards separated from the table –
commands are mostly issued via neural resonance or
subtle hand gestures.*

This desk is more than just a workstation. It's a symbiotic extension of the user's consciousness, designed to harmonize intellect, emotion and awareness. It reshapes itself based on task – flattening for drafting, curving for immersive simulations, or splitting into modular zones for collaboration.

In response to Faro's specific touching of the desk, his thought and vibration, the desk's reactive interface manifests the cosmic map as a hologram above the desk.

ITA

Why are these planets marked in
red?

FARO

Let's see. Their entire solar system is
caught in a high energy cloud.

ITA

Does it mean the entire solar system
is scheduled for ascension... or
destruction?

FARO

For sure, one of the two will happen.

ITA

What do we do about it?

FARO

We actively observe.

With her face in an inquisitive expression, without words, Ita poses her next question. Thus, Faro continues.

FARO (CONT'D)

Our supervising activities are many.
For example, we scan the thoughts
of the entire planetary population.
Then, via small UFOs, we transfer
those records every 24 hours to our
mothership, which sends that data
to its final destination. That way
we determine the evolution level,
therefore the capacity of each planet
and help them accordingly. We also
keep an eye on the geophysical status
of all planets exposed to energy that
is significantly stronger than the
energy those planets are used to.
We check on volcanos, earthquake-
prone areas, then weather patterns
and climate change – all of which can
be triggered as a global balancing
mechanism. However, if not taken
under control, the combination
of these elements could lead to a
planetary cataclysm.

ITA

Are these planets aware of the
thought recording and monitoring
system they are subjected to?

FARO

To know that, would be frightening
to them since they dwell in duality
consciousness. For that reason, our
constant benevolent supervision
cannot be explained to them. For the
time being, they could only see it as

an unjust interference into their free will.

ITA

Would they ever see it as a non-interference?

FARO

It will happen when they fully understand the natural and universal laws, and accept them as unquestionable and top rulers. Those laws are tried to be introduced to them firstly through the celestial stories about the power named God – its Divine Order and dominance over absolutely everything.

ITA

Clever.

FARO

Clever indeed but often slow. Hence some aeons-long efforts have been invested in human species. Where they are now in their evolution is not a coincidence. It is the result of celestial cultivation of their genetics, by the energies and the programmes they were exposed to.

Captain URROS is passing by.

He stops by Faro and Ita; gently putting his hand on Faro's shoulder.

CAPTAIN URROS

How is this young lady doing?

FARO

She keeps me busy with her
questions.

ITA

Captain Urros, if I may bother you –
this Cloud-X, we are observing now,
is a danger for the planets caught
in it – isn't it? Are those planets
powerless?

CAPTAIN URROS

The Cloud-X is a huge test and a
danger to them. Yet, have in mind
that the mother universe never
neglects its galaxies and planets.
Chances are always given to
assist those in a critical situation.
However, the final outcome, as
with everything, is in line with
the Universal Laws, which act
automatically. That means, there is
no favouritism.

ITA

Can the affected planets overcome
this demanding stage on their own?

CAPTAIN URROS

Their potential surely matches the
challenge. Cloud-X should trigger
that potential and hopefully we'll see

good development in no longer than 233 days – I think.

ITA

May I ask – why 233 days?

CAPTAIN URROS

It is the figure given by the Lords of Timing.

ITA

Fascinating!

CAPTAIN URROS

Well done, Ita! Curiosity is a sign of the mind eager to learn.

Captain Urros makes his move.

20. INT. CAMBRIDGE, MAX'S FLAT – NIGHT

Max and Tina are looking at the contents of the open fridge, and taking out some vegetables.

MAX

What are we going to cook tonight?

TINA

Let's do something in a wok – vegetables with tofu and rice noodles! Something like that?

MAX

Could not be better! What is my task?

                         TINA

        Your task could be to systematise the
        responses regarding Cloud-X that we
        have from across the globe, by using
        the findings of all social groups. I'll
        cook dinner meanwhile, and we'll
        take it from there.

                         MAX

        Amazing!

He kisses her gently and moves on toward his computer.

*Tina switches-on a music device and flows through the
kitchen.*

Joyfully busy, she sings and dances with the music.

21.   INT. CAMBRIDGE, MAX'S FLAT – NIGHT
      (CONTINUED)

*Just as Tina serves dinner, Max gets up and joins her in
the kitchen area.*

                         TINA

        Here you are!

                         MAX

        Woow! You are a magician!

They start their dinner.

                         MAX

        Delicious!

TINA

How about the job you were busy
with? Any findings?

MAX

It was not that big a job. Many online
friends are monitoring the responses
and some have even systematised
them.

TINA

Fascinating! A spontaneous sense of
concern and responsibility is globally
present! What have you discovered?

MAX

The first global surveys reveal one
far-prevailing idea as a solution to
this odd situation.

TINA

And, what is that suggestion?

MAX

Are you ready to hear it?

TINA

Of course.

MAX

Our generation voiced themselves in
a simple sentence: "Ask ET's to help
us".

TINA

YES! Why not accept that at one
level we are limited while on the
other – we are boundless! Why not
invite our extra-terrestrial friends to
help? It is so human-like to believe in
friendship! Great!

MAX

You are right – it is good to be aware
of one's own weaknesses in order
to know how to solve the problem
despite them. We all have many
weaknesses as well as strengths?
What do you think is our biggest
strength?

TINA

*(without thinking even a fraction of a
second)*

Love.

MAX

How about Logic?

TINA

Yes – the logic of the heart!

Both smile.

MAX

Interesting! By the way, do you think
our ET friends will give us a hand just
because we ask for it?

TINA

They will, if we deserve it according
to THEIR criteria.

MAX

Makes sense. Shall we organize a
global online meeting to chat with
friends from other countries?

TINA

I am so excited that we are moving
on.

22.   INT. GLOBAL ONLINE CONFERENCE

Youngsters are having a video conference:

GONZALES – MEXICO

As we all know, the tradition on this
planet is that the transfer of jobs and
duties from generation to generation
is gradual, almost unnoticeable.
However, at the moment things on
the planet have started to deviate
from that pattern. Our parents and
grandparents are becoming fully
dependent on others, unable to think
and care for themselves. It seems
they are losing their compatibility
with the energy of time.

GITA – INDIA

*As Gita speaks, we watch a video illustration of the
youth activity she describes.*

We, here in India, are already
working on establishing special
institutions, lake care homes for
those affected and are just about
to get fully public on the topic. We
are also starting to liaise with the
government. We want our elders
to know that we are aware of the
challenge and will not neglect them –
no matter what.

KIO – JAPAN

Impressive activity, Gita. I think it is
necessary to engage in such projects,
regardless of the fact that the
solution expressed by our generation
is to ask ETs to help the planet.

VIMBO – ZIMBABWE

I agree. We should not just wait
for ETs to step in and remedy the
situation. We have a responsibility
towards our parents and
grandparents. Besides, we cannot
even know whether we deserve ETs
friendly intervention. How could
we know that? We can only hope,
or even believe – but, in any case,
should not just sit and wait.

TATIANA – RUSSIA

*As Tatiana speaks, we watch a video illustration of
youth activity in Russia.*

I believe that the universe is a totality
that self-regulates all its aspects. It
means, our concerns and ideas to

help our elders are what the universe is whispering to our hearts and minds to do. Here in Russia, we are initiating information campaigns and are working on defining key support strategies, both on how to offer the best care and how to compensate for the lack of working staff across all sectors.

ASAN – EGYPT

We, the generation of youth on this planet, claim the authority to decide about our future. We support the invitation to ETs to help us as soon as possible.

HUGO – SWEDEN

The generation of our parents and their parents have not realised how globally connected the members of the new generations are, and that we do not just play computer games with friends across the continents. We are watchful and patient with the older generations. We love and respect them our way. We are awaiting our time to show that. And it seems, that time is now.

DAVID – USA

Exactly. We have a chance now to work together, globally, on a most serious project, far beyond entertainment. All our skills and virtues will be tested. I do not think that we even have a choice.

RICHARD – AUSTRALIA

The time in front of us might be extremely traumatic, but that cannot be an excuse for escaping our responsibility. We cannot simply hand it to the ETs. Having said that, it does not mean I am against ETs benevolent intervention. They should know that they are more than welcome to help.

TINA – UK

So great to hear from you all, guys. I am impressed. As many have mentioned, it is better not to put all our eggs in one basket. Indeed, it will be amazing if ETs help us, but they might not do so before we explore and exhaust all our potentials first.

JORN – HOLLAND

Perhaps, we could ask spiritually aware friends across the planet to invest in visions of positive outcomes from the current global situation?

MAX – UK

Brilliant idea. I'll make sure to contribute. By the way, my grandmother used to say: "God always helps, but not until the last moment." So, as Tina suggested – let us explore our potential in this beautiful collaboration! I am so excited.

23.   INT. LONDON, CONFERENCE ROOM – DAY

A small conference room on a high up floor, with a panoramic view of iconic London buildings.

IAN (MI5) plus 6 social media platform representatives – are all seated around an oval table.

IAN

We, in the internal affairs department, have felt the need to include you, the representatives of social media platforms in this discussion. Thank you for coming. The idea for this meeting came after witnessing the flood of social media activities related to the slogan "Save our parents and grandparents". What is very concerning is the global proportion of this motion and, in particular, the appearance of the suggestion "Ask ETs to help us". This sentence dominates all social media platforms ... And it seems, it has been posed by our youngsters.

REPRESENTATIVE 1

What percentage of the population are those below 36?

IAN

Regardless of how massive they are as a social group, and how active and influential they are on social platforms, they cannot have authority for such an action!!! They have to be stopped.

REPRESENTATIVE 2

What do you mean stopped?

IAN

I mean what I've just said: they cannot invite unknown celestial entities to directly intervene on this planet, and trust in their benevolence. It does not make sense.

REPRESENTATIVE 3 – MRS HALL

Why should we not trust ETs?

IAN

Because ETs are not to be trusted.

REPRESENTATIVE 3 – MRS HALL

I am afraid, that is not an answer. What are your arguments? Are you primed by long negative propaganda regarding ETs?

REPRESENTATIVE 4

Hold on, Miss Hall. It is an ugly assumption. As far as I understand, we are talking about planetary interest here and have to elevate our viewpoint.

REPRESENTATIVE 3 – MRS HALL

That is exactly what I expect us to do. And if anybody is entertaining assumptions – that is You, Mr. Taylor

IAN

I'd rather we spend our time generating some constructive ideas in the given planetary situation. Are there any?

REPRESENTATIVE 4

Sure, I have one: close the access to social media platforms to those who are spreading the slogan "Ask ETs to help us".

24. INT. SPACECRAFT MANNA-373, MEETING ROOM – DAY

A meeting at a room named "Pressing Issues".

Seven people are present. On the agenda: the PLANET EARTH.

As Person 1 speaks, his words are illustrated with relevant scenes from across planet Earth.

PERSON 1

On planet Earth, a mass memory loss and an impediment of the thought mechanism amongst the population above the age of 50 is being witnessed. These individuals become dysfunctional and have to leave their professional posts. They retire either at special care homes or at private homes, where their children care for them. Due to the lack of staff, production of goods and services will almost stop; then food will also become scarce. This tendency will lead the entire planetary population into survival mode.

On the other hand, the youth on the planet is organising themselves increasingly more and more in the search for a solution. Their focus is on us. They openly seek our intervention to stop the oncoming civilizational collapse.

PERSON 2

We are not obliged to help them! Why would we do that? When the planet I come from was going through a major ascension, we were left to our own selves!

PERSON 1

How can you be so sure that the Universal Federation did not help? Is it because we did not land on your planet to acknowledge our action? You are forgetting that the Cosmic Federation does not do power demonstrations. We do not need to fascinate any planet or galaxy with our capabilities. Do you still think we should not help planet Earth?

PERSON 2

Yes, I do. Because I also do not think human beings benefit when OTHERS solve their problem? Problems are encountered in order to learn to solve them using one's own potential, and gradually become able to withstand the energy of even the most adverse situations. This learning to harmonise with all energies that are on people's evolutionary plate, is an important factor which evolves them.

25.   EXT. CAMBRIDGE, CAM RIVER – DAY

Tina and Max are in a small boat floating on the river Cam.

Fully present, they soak in the tranquil beauty of the moment.

                          TINA

            Who is going to love us when all
            our parents, aunts, uncles and
            grandparents, lose their memory,
            forget who they are and who we are
            to them? Who is going to adore us?

                          MAX

            We are always loved!

                          TINA

            What do you mean?

                          MAX

            It is not just love of our parents that
            brought us into existence and keeps
            us going.

TINA

Of course, our friends love us, our boyfriends!?

MAX

You are right, but there is more to it...
Originally, we were created before
our terrestrial parents conceived
us! Our parents just contributed in
perpetuating human reproduction.
However, the Human Being as well as
the entire Creation are designed and
manifested by the Great Power – that
cannot even be named. Each and
every particle carries an aspect of
that Power – carries Love.

TINA

Are you saying that every particle in creation loves all other particles?

MAX

Exactly! Our cells love plants,
animals, minerals... on the other
hand; the entirety of Nature
emanates the frequency of love. No
wonder, we feel nourished when we
are in nature.

TINA

Are you saying we are to love all and
everything – even cockroaches?!
Hmm, I am not sure about that one. I
am not there yet!

Both smile.

MAX

You'll be there. Unconditional love
is within the vibratory scope of our
cells. It is an attribute of our DNA. As
we get closer to the essence of who
we are, the more unconditional is the
love we experience. We accept and
love everything equally – eventually
even cockroaches. No discrimination
whatsoever.

TINA

You keep fascinating me with your
knowledge. How have you acquired
it?

MAX

I don't really know. All I was doing
was looking to find myself... and...

TINA

And?

MAX

I found you!

Both smile in mutual affection.

Tina naughtily scoops some river water and quickly
splashes Max several times.

In reaction, smiles turn into a happy, joyous amusement
of splashing water at each other.

MAX (CONT'D)

I found love, then discovered that we
are love-powered batteries capable

of self-charge. We can generate love vibrations by our own will, by our mere conscious choices. Not only that but our love also feeds our near and dear ones, and the universes as well.

TINA

If we are so powerful, why don't we use that power to protect our parents and grandparents from losing their memory? We shall test the power of love and how powerful we are!

MAX

As a matter of fact, we are always tested on love. For example, start with me and my parents! There is a huge gap between my view and their views... I need to practice acceptance, patience and tolerance all the time – and, in actuality, it is LOVE that provides those.

TINA

You are right.

MAX

Parents, of course, stick to the values they revere and to their occasionally patronising attitude – mostly because their starting premise is that, since they have lived longer in this lifetime, they have more experience and are more knowledgeable, and therefore should be listened to.

TINA

Yes. My parents are not much different, and our communication is not always smooth. However, I do not blame them for being as they are. I believe they always do their best. If any time they could do better, I trust they would do it. They have an instinctive drive to care about their offspring; do they not?

MAX

You are right, but sometimes I think that it would be easier to come to common terms with ETs than with my parents.

TINA

By the way, any sign of any ETs noticing our invitation to help us?

MAX

Not that I am aware of. But, let's see.

Max takes his mobile phone from his pocket, and looks for some information.

MAX

The stream of our requests goes on.

MAX (CONT'D)

(he reads)

"We don't want to lose ourparents
and grandparent; we do not want
them to suffer.

ETs, we believe you can help us and
you will."

Messages continue to arrive. Max looks at Tina.

MAX (CONT'D)

Let's continue testing the power of love!

26. EXT. BRAZIL, REMOTE COUNTRYSIDE,
     VILLAGE RESIDENCE OF A SHAMAN – DAY

*We see a shaman's ranch and Bruno sitting across a
native shaman.*

BRUNO

Could you please tell me more about
what you told me recently when I
visited you?

SHAMAN

It was not me who was
communicating with you. So, I cannot
recall what I said to you. I am just
an instrument, a channel, of the
spiritual world we do not see. So,
my willingness to be at your service
is not the guarantee that you will be
given a relevant message.

BRUNO

I see.

SHAMAN

(goes into a meditative state... soon, he speaks)

Any guidance, but the one from your essence, can mislead you.

After a prolonged silence, the shaman returns from his meditative state.

BRUNO

(in a highly restrained mode – neither pleased nor displeased)

Sure, well said...thank you.

27.   EXT. NIGERIA, REMOTE VILLAGE – DAY

Aabi is with a babalawo, an Odu IFA divinator, and eager to hear what the world of spirit has to tell him about the automatic writing he experienced recently.

Babalawo uses 16 sacred nuts and a wooden divination tray carved on its edges. He throws the nuts four times to obtain sixteen combinations.

After completing that stage, he speaks:

IFA DIVINATOR

It is up to you to understand your experiences.

It is up to you to see behind the veil of separation.

It is up to you to discern the truth.

                    AABI

          (he utters it more for himself)
Oh, well...

28.   INT. CHINA, BUDDHIST TEMPLE – DAY

Chen meets a Buddhist monk in a small temple.

Both are seated in a lotus position.

                    MONK

          We are aware of an ongoing
          communication between dimensions.
          It can be through the direct open
          channel of a person, then through
          telepathic transfers, inspiration,
          intuition, sacred teachings or dreams.

                    CHEN

          I see. I never thought of those as
          the means of interdimensional
          communication. But – it makes
          sense.

                    MONK

          Many things and experiences are not
          what we think they are.

                    CHEN

          What about our dreams? Recently,
          I had a very disturbing dream
          regarding the whole of humanity on

this planet. I am not sure how to look at it.

MONK

Dreaming is your personal experience based on your brain activity, after the brain switches off from the terrestrial vibrational medium. Your etheric body leaves the visible physical body, goes up and experiences ...

Monk makes a pause.

Both men are silent.

CHEN

Does it make sense to remember and analyse our dreams?

MONK

It is difficult to say a general statement such as – it is good to remember our dreams. If we say so, people could become obsessed with the most insignificant parts of their dreams and become paralysed in their daily activities. In other words, dreams should not be promoted to the level of prophecy – but, mind you, I am not saying that dreams cannot come true.

CHEN

I see. Nothing is really simple.

MONK

Regarding dreams, one thing though IS SIMPLE – a heavy meal late at night will keep your etheric body closer to the terrestrial vibrational level.

They laugh.

The monk continues in his most genuine manner.

MONK (CONT'D)

Then comes a dream full of difficulties, since your digestive system is busy processing and sorting out the food you ingested. It is as if you loaded your pockets with lots of stones while trying to fly on your own wings. Instead of ascending to enjoy beautiful vistas, you drop into the sea, face dangerous creatures there... and spend the rest of the dream trying to escape them.

CHEN

Thank you. You have said a lot, but I am not sure you helped me. Perhaps, I am now more confused than I was before asking you anything.

MONK

The more confused you are – the better. You are closer to the solution; you are closer to the realisation that the most useful help is found inside you and it is always available. Dare to go for it. See what yourself has to tell

you. Be honest – otherwise it will not
work.

29.   INT. MAX'S FLAT – NIGHT

Max and Tina are seated by his computer.

*Max scrolls down along the seemingly endless list of
letters to celestials and stops at one of them.*

We see it on the screen while an off-screen voice reads:

MALE NARRATOR (V.O.)

- *Dear celestial family. I know you exist, and our
  connection has never ceased. I believe you
  care about us, yet you let us make mistakes
  and suffer in the process of learning and
  growing. I believe you never wish to witness
  the extinction of human life on Earth, and
  you have the capacity to help the part of our
  planetary population, which is directly affected
  with the current time energy.*
- *If the Universal Laws allow you to intervene in
  cases as ours, we are giving you authority to
  do so.*
- *By saving us, all will benefit – all of Creation
  will benefit.*

MAX

Here is an interesting one, directly
addressed to God.

We see it on the screen while an off-screen voice reads.

FEMALE NARRATOR (V.O.)

Dear God,

If this is your wish to rid the planet of older people, so be it. I say so because I trust in the best intention of all your programmes, trust in your unceasing benevolence. It will be a painful process, but we will have to go through it. However, that is not the point. If they are gone, the only parent we would have is YOU. Are you doing all this to return us to a full alignment with You, because we might have deviated from your guidance? I am not disputing your plans and ways. Whatever they are, you can count on my faithful respect of your will.

MAX

What a consciousness! What a level of love!

30. INT. OXFORD COLLEGE, HEAD OF DEPARTMENT OFFICE – DAY

Mark and Kevin are at the office of the Head of their department, Mr GIBSON:

MARK

Mr Gibson, you are aware of our work on Cloud-X.

MR GIBSON

Indeed. What about it? Do you need more funds?

KEVIN

No, Mr Gibson. The challenge is of a different nature.

MR GIBSON

Such as?

MARK

There are some potentially devastating effects related to the Cloud-X! People of a certain age have problems in thinking and memorizing. The same symptoms are evident worldwide.

MR GIBSON

Why do you connect those two things?

KEVIN

A good question. The rationale is actually very simple: since this specific health deterioration is very recent and global, the cause must be global. The energy of Cloud-X is therefore a most logical culprit.

MARK

Ultimately, this new energy could disable the entire world population above the age of 50. We have evidence of such a trend. People are noticing this and we think they deserve to know the truth.

MR GIBSON

Are you suggesting to announce to
the whole world that Cloud-X causes
that problem?

KEVIN

Yes, because we believe that the
right solution might only be born
from interdisciplinary and global
collaborations.

MR GIBSON

I do not see how knowing about
Cloud-X can be useful to people, so
we will only communicate about it
through scientific papers.

MARK

Can we at least ...

Abrupt interference quickly concludes this conversation.

MR GIBSON

Was I not clear enough? So, I will
repeat: No Cloud-X public disclosure
outside the scientific community!

31.   INT. OXFORD COLLEGE, CORRIDOR – DAY

*Kevin and Mark in the corridor immediately after
leaving Mr Gibson's office:*

KEVIN

Mark, what are we going to do?

MARK

I do not care what Mr Gibson thinks,
I will do what my entire being is
leading me to do.

KEVIN

But it might be dangerous.

MARK

It is dangerous to live! Is it not?

32. INT. INTERNET TV CHANEL PREMISES –
     NIGHT

TV studio.

Mark and the TV host are ready to go live.

The short interview begins.

TV HOST (MALE)

Good evening! Our guest tonight is
Mark Barrnet, the senior lecturer
at the department of astrophysics...
Good evening, Mr Barnet, and thanks
for coming to our studio. What is
it you wanted to share with our
audience tonight?

MARK

Thanks for having me in your show.
Usually, we scientists do not go
around to broadcasting companies
to inform a wide audience about our
findings. However, this time, I am
deeply motivated to do exactly that. I

wish people to know the real reason behind the unusual symptoms of sudden memory loss and impaired thinking that are being observed globally in certain population segments. I am afraid, I am not in a position to offer a solution to this misfortune at this moment, but I can name the cause of it – which is a valuable starting point.

TV HOST

What is the cause, Mr Barrett?

MARK

According to our findings, our solar system has entered an interstellar cloud that is dramatically influencing the vibrational rate of the energy on Earth. Some scientists relate the symptoms mentioned to the alteration of the energy on Earth caused by this cloud – and I am one of them.

TV HOST

Mr Barrett, what do you suggest in the given circumstances?

MARK

I can only suggest that as many as possible scientists, of all branches, from across the planet, join their brain powers and work on finding a solution.

TV HOST

If you are right, Mr Barrett, if your
conclusions are correct, the situation
on the planet is rather scary. The
challenge at hand seems colossal.

MARK

I agree. The truth is sometimes bitter.
However, it is good to know it, since
the truth directs our action in the
right direction and prevents us from
wasting time.

TV HOST

Thanks for this intriguing
information, Mr Barrett. I hope it
will have a constructive impact on
people. Any concluding message to
our audience?

MARK

Keep calm. Panic will be least
useful. Organize yourselves in your
communities, in your professional
and other groups. Help those in
need. Even if something looks
devastating, in a bigger context it
might lead to a beautiful outcome.
Thus, stay optimistic – no matter
what.

33.   INT. INTERNET TV CHANEL PREMISES –
      NIGHT (CONTINUED)

Mark is still in the TV station premises.

Accompanied by the TV interview host, Mark is moving toward the exit of the building.

TV HOST

Thanks for your courage, Mr
Barrett, to share such vital planetary
information in front of the cameras.
I need some time to digest what you
disclosed tonight.

MARK

I hope all will be fine with you, since
you dared to host me in your show.
Stay in touch.

The TV host opens the door.

Mark steps out onto the street.

It is raining heavily.

34.   EXT./INT. OXFORD – STREET – NIGHT
(CONTINUED)

Strong rain.

Mark is entering his car after the TV interview.

We follow him driving slowly, while deeply in his thoughts.

After a while, he switches his radio on. Classical music.

He eventually parks his car in the private driveway of a cosy house on the outskirts of Oxford.

While still inside the car, his mobile phone rings and he picks up the call.

BRENDA (V.O.)

Hi, this is Brenda, Mr Gibson's
secretary. May I speak to Mr Barrett?

MARK

Speaking. Hi, Brenda.

BRENDA (V.O.)

Mr Barrett, I am sorry for disturbing
you at this late hour. I was asked by
Mr Gibson to inform you to come to
collect your redundancy letter and
all your belongings from the College
premises.

MARK

Thank you, Brenda.

Mark shows no sign of a shock.

*He switches-off the car radio and stays a few minutes
inside the car.*

35.   INT. MARK'S HOUSE – NIGHT (CONTINUED)

*Wet from the rain, Mark is entering the house where
he lives with her partner ZOE.*

ZOE

Hi. You are late.

MARK

Sorry, I had an unexpected meeting.
How was your day?

ZOE

I was busy as usual. Nothing really
special. How about you?

MARK

I am afraid, I do not have good news
to share.

ZOE

Sorry?

MARK

I do not know whether you could
understand, but a strange chain of
circumstances led to me losing my
job at university. I was just informed.

ZOE

What do you mean? What "strange
chain of circumstances"?

MARK

It is really complicated to explain.

ZOE

Are you really saying you managed to
let your career slip away just like that.
How are we going to survive without
your salary? You are so irresponsible!
How could you do this to me?

MARK

It has nothing to do with you.

ZOE

That is exactly what I am pointing out: you obviously did not think about me or us at all, while doing what you did.

MARK

I have to admit – I did not. But it all went so fast and my focus was on humanity – not on any individual, not even me or us.

ZOE

Then, how can you claim that you love me?

MARK

You know I do. Nothing has changed in that respect.

ZOE

My God! I need some time to process this situation. You will help if you moved out, and leave me alone as soon as possible.

MARK

Zoe, are you sure?

ZOE

Oh yes. I am very sure.

MARK

How can you be so sure so quickly?
May I say that NOW I AM the one
who is surprised.

ZOE

Look, you are telling me that you are
surprised! What am I then? I am truly
and utterly shocked.

MARK

I see. I will organize myself and leave
the house as soon as I can.

Zoe leaves the living room in a dramatic way, making more noise with the doors than needed.

With indifference, Mark observes yet another sudden development in his life.

Slowly, as if carrying a huge burden on his shoulders, he walks into his office room.

36.   INT. MARK'S HOUSE – NIGHT (CONTINUED)

Mark is in his office room.

A white envelope on his desk immediately attracts his attention. We see him opening it and taking a letter out.

Still standing by his desk, Mark reads the letter.

UNKNOWN (V.O.)

Those who think that intelligent life
in the universe is on this planet only,
need to expand their awareness. The

universe is bursting with intelligent life on numberless planets, some of which are a mirror-image of this world. There are also planets more evolved technologically, morally and ethically. They are ready to help your world, as soon as you amicably accept their existence and their currently superior position over you. If you fear them as dangerous enemies of your planet, you decide which reality you will experience. For, what you entertain in your thoughts are the vibrational prescriptions for the events/reality you are inviting to your life. You create a different reality, based on whether you dwell in fear, or love and light.

Mark finally sits in his desk-chair and continues reading.

UNKNOWN (V.O.) (CONT'D)

This civilization has much to lose and much to gain – all depending on whether you are ready to unite globally and work together for the benefits of all. If you can, you will reconnect with your celestial family and find yourself at the place you have always been dreaming about.

The scenario based on humans whose essence is locked, who see ETs as bad, cannot go on anymore. We are awaiting your choice to stop projecting on all ETs your own helplessness, aggressiveness, and the need to control and exploit.

Wake up humanity!

Wake up, and step into the next level
of your power by conquering your
fears and conditionings.

You are in control of your destiny.
Your choices create your future.

Mark finishes reading, keeps the letter in his hands for a while.

He gets up, opens the window and stands in front of it.

Strong rain is still washing his garden and Mark lets it do so with his thoughts, as if to wash away from his mind the surreal events of the day.

37.   INT. MARK'S HOUSE – NEXT DAY, MORNING

Zoe has just finished her breakfast and is drinking her coffee in the kitchen.

Mark enters the kitchen with the mysterious letter in his hand.

MARK

Good morning.

Zoe is silent.

MARK (CONT'D)

Sorry for all inconvenience caused.
I have packed some of my things
and am moving out after breakfast.
Daniel was kind enough to offer me
to stay at his place.

                              ZOE

Thank you.

                             MARK

I've found an envelope at my desk. It
doesn't have a stamp or any sign of
being handled by the post office. Do
you remember who brought it?

                              ZOE

No, I don't.

Zoe gets up and leaves the kitchen area.

*We follow her taking her bag, checking her image
in the mirror at the house entrance and opening the
external door.*

                        ZOE (CONT'D)

I am off.

*Mark turns the letter upside down and writes on the
back of it:*

                        MARK (O.S.)

"As it seems, nobody has brought this
letter to my office! I better stop being
surprised with anything anymore and
start believing that impossible things
happen!"

38.   EXT. / INT. DANIEL'S HOUSE – THE SAME DAY,
      LATER

The doorbell rings.

Daniel opens the door and sees Mark with a suitcase and backpack.

DANIEL

Here you are! Welcome.

MARK

Thanks for offering me to stay with
you and your family. It is so kind. I
hope I will not bother you for long.

DANIEL

Thanks for accepting the offer. We
will cope with you – don't worry.

They laugh.

Mark leaves his belongings at the entrance corridor.

They enter the living room.

Tina is there, busy feeding the fish in a massive aquarium.

DANIEL

Tina, this is Mark – my friend from
my university days. He will stay with
us for a while.

MARK

Nice to meet you, Tina. I see, you
have a fabulous collection of deep-
sea creatures. Look at those corals!

Mark comes close to the aquarium to admire its inhabitants.

As feeding time is still on, even those creatures that spend time hiding behind the rocks or in the sand, are out and about.

We enjoy the display of colours and movements.

TINA

Thanks, Mark. Nice to meet you too. Are you concerned with the situation on the planet!? I certainly am – as well as many of my friends across the globe. We think it is a good idea to lobby the government to secure funds for additional elderly homes; for education in care and for global scientific research. If you are a scientist, you could perhaps lobby for the funding regarding science.

MARK

I AM VERY MUCH CONCERNED about humanity, but fundraising is not my field of expertise. I understand the sky but not the government.

TINA

See, I am not a nurse either but, as it seems, I will have to become one soon. I am sure you know how to make a phone call, how to write an email or find the relevant contacts – so you are already well qualified for the task.

39.   INT. OXFORD OFFICE BUILDING – DAY

Zoe is working at her office shared with two other colleagues.

Her phone rings.

ZOE

Hi Dad! How are you?

ZOE'S FATHER (V.O.)

Darling, I am fine but your mother
is unwell. Could you please come to
visit us over the weekend?

ZOE

What's wrong?

We see Zoe listening and changing her facial expression to one consumed by shock.

ZOE (CONT'D)

See you, Dad.

40.   INT. ZOE'S PARENTS FAMILY HOUSE – DAY

Zoe's mother's bedroom.

Visibly absent-minded, the old woman is sitting on her bed.

Occasionally, she seems eager to communicate yet without a capacity to perceive correctly, or to think and to process information.

Distressed, Zoe is still finding a way to comfort her mom.

ZOE

Mom, EVERYTHING will be fine...
everything...

41.   EXT. DANIEL'S HOUSE GARDEN – DAY

Daniel and Mark are sitting in the garden.

After finishing a mobile phone conversation, Mark returns his attention to Daniel.

DANIEL

It seems as if after your TV interview, you lost your job but gained on popularity – globally. Isn't it so interesting: losing on one side seemed necessary for gaining on the other.

MARK

Exactly. The Law of Equilibrium never fails. I have to admit, I am surprised with the number of scientists and people on different walks of life who have contacted me since. They wish to contribute and help in any way possible. As a matter of fact, I have been liaising with a number of scientists and have good news! A colleague from the US is organizing a multidisciplinary science conference on Cloud-X. I plan to attend.

DANIEL

Sounds promising.

Pause.

DANIEL (CONT'D)

By the way, how is Zoe?

MARK

I have not disturbed her since I left.
I understood she wanted solitude to
think over everything.

At that very instant, Mark's mobile phone rings.

MARK (CONT'D)

(to Daniel)

Gosh, it is Zoe! Do you mind if I pick
up this call?

DANIEL

Sure. I'll leave you alone.

MARK

Thanks.

Daniel gets up and moves towards the house.

Mark picks up the call.

MARK (CONT'D)

Hi Zoe.

Zoe is crying uncontrollably.

ZOE

Hi.

MARK

What is going on?

ZOE

When are you returning?

MARK

I do not know.

ZOE

Please, forgive me for being so
unreasonable when I asked you to
leave.

MARK

That is OK, Zoe. I understand. It was a
moment when I was also not able to
think straight.

ZOE

Darling, I love you.

MARK

Why are you crying? You can stop –
you know that I love you too.

ZOE

My mother, my mother has lost her
capacity to speak clearly.

MARK

Sorry to hear that.

                    ZOE

When will you come back?

                    MARK

I am afraid, I am engaged at some
professional gathering for next
couple of days, and will return when
I can.

                    ZOE

Again!

                    MARK

What do you mean AGAIN?

                    ZOE

Again, something else is between me
and you.

                    MARK

Depends on how you choose to see
it.

42.   INT. CAMBRIDGE, CAFFE SHOP – DAY

*Max is sitting in a café accompanied by his tall artist
friend, OLIVER, from London.*

                    MAX

Do you know why I have invited you?

                    OLIVER

To catch up with me.

MAX

Of course, but there are some other reasons. Knowing your international artists network, I thought it would be great to activate it for the pressing planetary needs.

OLIVER

What are you talking about?

MAX

I've spent lots of time thinking how to be the most effective, since strange things are happening to some people around the world.

OLIVER

What strange things? Which people? Man, can you stop being so secretive and tell me what it is all about?

MAX

It is a long story. I will tell you later. However, in tackling the issue at hand, we need a constant wave of positive energy across the planet. To be more effective, perhaps, we should organize into meditation groups. Our mental efforts will then amplify.

OLIVER

Sure. Let's do that! I like triangles. How about if the number of people in a group is a multiple of 3.

So: 3 could be the smallest group, or a core of a bigger group. If each one of 3 friends finds 6 more people – it will become a group of 21 brains – 7 triangles! How does it sound to you? Is it too complicated?

MAX

I love it. So, we already work in groups of 3 in our action-areas. I knew we'll work as one. When it comes to saving humanity, to me, nothing is complicated or too demanding. But, if the 21-configuration is too complex to some people, let's organise in groups of 18.

OLIVER

Sounds good to me.

MAX

Let's start networking and introducing this operational concept to our friends across the world?

OLIVER

Hold on! You promised to explain why all this, and why such a rush.

MAX

Look, Tina, my girlfriend, has organised a gathering at my place at 7.

He checks the time on his mobile.

MAX (CONT'D)

It's nearly 7 now. Why don't you join
us and stay overnight at my place?
I guess, you do not need to hurry
back to London because tomorrow is
Sunday.

OLIVER

I definitely cannot go home before
I've found out what I agreed to put
myself into.

*They get up and move towards the exit of the coffee
shop.*

43.   INT. MAX'S FLAT – EVENING

*Max, Tina, Oliver, MAGGY, ANN, KATE and JOSH – all
about the same age – are comfortably scattered across
Max's open space living room area.*

*Empty buffet-style arranged dishes and used paper
plates are in the kitchen section.*

MAX

Who doesn't have a drink?

OLIVER

Hot water, please.

TINA

Herbal tea for me, thank you Max.

MAGGY

Shall we sum up our plan of action?
Tina, do you mind starting?

TINA

Ok. Here we go... our group of 3
has applied for a one-million-pound
fund for new care homes and are
absolutely thrilled about it. Another
group of 3, which Maggy works in,
is now focusing on choosing the
most suitable prefabricated type of
building that we could use. They are
also looking for available locations
across the country, where those new
care homes will be erected as soon
as possible. In our third group of 3
friends, Ann is busy training carers
for new care homes.

OLIVER

Woow, guys!

TINA

Hold on, Oliver. That's not all. Groups
of 3 people are mushrooming on
all continents where they replicate
this scheme. Like us here, they are
working on building new nursing
homes and providing trained staff to
run them. So, we have become global
– because, clearly, our generation is
ready and capable to cooperate on
that scale. Isn't it?

JOSH

I am the technical support, and I also work with 2 friends to manage IT issues.

KATE

My group of 3 is covering our social media presence, regarding all activities that Tina has mentioned, and we work closely with Josh's group.

MAX

On the map of our activities, I am in the steering group of 3 who follow the global movement we named "Ask ETs to help us".

OLIVER

ETs! How are you going to get in touch with them and tell them that? Do you have a cosmic password?

MAX

I think we do not need it. You know, even in the sacred books, given more than a thousand years ago, it was declared "God is closer to you than your aorta". To me, it reads that all about us, our thoughts and deeds, is known up there.

Max looks up as if to make sure to convey that help is expected from outside Earth.

MAX (CONT'D)

(to Oliver)

Does that make sense to you?

OLIVER

It does NOW, but it did not until this very moment.

They all laugh.

ANN

Fast learner!

TINA

If we may know, is there anything Oliver is willing to help us with?

MAX

As far as I understand, Oliver is eager to join our efforts and help us –

OLIVER

– and feels privileged to do so.

MAT

We discussed the format of his and our work.

OLIVER

Thanks for inviting me to such a noble action. So interesting that you are organising yourselves in groups of 3 – like the ancient Romans did with their TRIUMVIRATES. I also believe that having an operational SYSTEM

— is a more effective way of investing
our energy than doing something
spontaneously. I know, it comes as
a surprise since I am an artist – but,
what shall I say, artists are here to
break the patterns!

Olive offers his warm smile.

OLIVER (CONT'D)

Max and I have decided to organize
meditation groups, of 18 and 21
friends, across our country and
expand the concept globally. I will
focus on networking and spreading
the word about the current need for
this kind of unification and action.
Along the way, Max will provide more
detailed information and advice to
those interested to join.

TINA

FANTASTIC! We need the community
of artists to step in, in a bigger
number. But, of course, anybody is
welcome.

*An abrupt knocking at the entrance door immediately
grounds all 7 friends.*

*Speechless, they exchange puzzling looks at one
another.*

TINA

Max, are you expecting anybody?

MAX

Not that I am aware of.

44.   INT/EXT. MAX'S FLAT – NIGHT (CONTINUED)

Mark at the flat's main entrance.

Outside, we see two civilians showing their identity cards to Max.

We do not hear their conversation.

45.   INT. MAX'S FLAT – NIGHT (CONTINUED)

Max is back in the living room flooded by a deep and puzzling silence.

> MAX
>
> I am invited for an interrogation
> at the local police station. Officers
> showed me an interrogation warrant
> but could not tell anything more.

> TINA
>
> It must be a mistake. Shall I come
> with you?

> MAX
>
> No need for that. Don't worry. I'll be
> back soon.

Max kisses Tina.

> MAX (CONT'D)
>
> *(with no agitation in his voice)*
>
> Guys, carry on the good work.

In one long glance, Max makes eye contact with most of his guests and leaves.

46. INT. CAMBRIDGE, POLICE STATION – NIGHT
    (CONTINUED)

POLICEMAN

You are Max Gosh, are you not?

MAX

Yes, I am.

POLICEMAN

We have evidence that you are
leading a campaign to invite ETs to
intervene on this planet.

MAX

I am one of those, Sir.

POLICEMAN

Are you not aware of the danger of
such an approach?

MAX

I am.

POLICEMAN

Why do you do it then?

MAX

Because, the fact that some ETs can
harm us does not mean there are
no others who are there to help. If
we ask for help, they might even
be obliged to deliver it. You cannot
prove otherwise, can you?

POLICEMAN

What makes you believe you are
inviting only the good ones?

MAX

I am afraid, Sir, I do not think I can
describe this to you. It is a matter
of belief, and beliefs cannot be
rationalized.

POLICEMAN

Young man, you are not invited here
to philosophise.

MAX

I am aware of it. However, I am
only telling you my truth. If it is not
compatible with the view of those
who ordered this interrogation –
what can I do.

POLICEMAN

Max Gosh, I am afraid, our
conversation seems to be going
nowhere. I have to keep you
overnight here and, tomorrow, my
colleague will deal with you.

MAX

I see.

POLICEMAN

Follow me, please.

Max gets up and is escorted to a detention room.

                    POLICEMAN

Can you please empty all your
pockets.

*Max checks his pockets and takes out his mobile phone
only.*

                        MAX

I need my mobile with me.

                    POLICEMAN

That is not in line with our policy. You
should hand it to me.

                        MAX

I need to inform my girlfriend about
what happened.

                    POLICEMAN

We can do it for you – if you wish.

                        MAX

Please.

Max does as he is instructed.

*The policeman takes his mobile phone and locks him
up.*

47.   INT. MAX'S FLAT – NIGHT (CONTINUED)

Max's home – just after Max was taken away.

*Tina, Maggy, Kate, Ann, Josh and Oliver are trying to
make sense of what has just happened.*

OLIVER

So, they will keep Max overnight. How should we interpret that?

TINA

The only thing I could think of is that Max's activities related to our "Ask ET's to help us" initiative are a problem. Since lots of coordination in that respect is done from Max's computer – he was identified and summoned up.

MAGGY

But summoned up for what?

ANN

Who knows what the authorities might not like about it!

JOSH

Maybe it is all about authority – because, at the moment, it is us, the young generation, who is assuming authority to decide the future of this planet.

KATE

Which means – they do not trust us.

MAGGY

They gave us their genes, why would they not trust us?

ANN

If our parents do not trust us, who
are their kids, do they trust in
themselves or anybody else?

JOSH

I am really not sure why it is like
that. For example, they still don't
understand that if we wish, we
can demonstrate our power on
the internet, as a generation. It is
a domain where we are like fish in
water. We can always easily out-
manoeuvre them by generating
campaigns beyond what they can
imagine.

MAGGY

Why don't we do that?

*With their eyes wide open, everyone is looking at
others, as if asking permission for an act of that kind.*

Not uttered yet, an agreement is felt in the air.

48.   GLOBAL ACTIVITIES

*We see social platforms flooded with support for Max
Gosh.*

*Multiple screens feature different social media and
the endless stream of the SINGLE message: "I am Max
Gosh".*

*In no time, the message also appears in the
computers and social media accounts of corporations,*

governmental institutions, universities, namely –
EVERYWHERE.

Unstoppably, this simple statement is conquering internet space globally, even though anti-hacking teams worldwide work hard to get rid of the intruding message.

As they try to solve the problem, an increasing number of people investigate who Max Gosh is. Thus, the awareness, about the difficult planetary situation and about the invitation of ETs to help, also increases.

49.   INT. MAX'S FLAT – NEXT DAY – MORNING

Oliver is sleeping on the sofa bed in the living room in Max's flat.

Tina is sitting by Max's computer.

We see her writing directly to her social media platform, while her voice reading her message aloud to us.

TINA (V.O.)

Dear parents and grandparents, ETs
will help us. You cannot stop that
by detaining one of us. We are each
a Max Gosh – so no way you can
disable us all. As a matter of fact, we
can easily disable your position that
you consider powerful. We can – but
another thing is whether we want to
do it. Please, have in mind that no
data of yours is secure! Wake up to
that truth!

We understand your uneasiness
and your obsolete ways. You need

help and we are offering it to you. Whether you understand it or not – but without us, in the given circumstances, you hardly have a future.

Come on, our parents and grandparents! Do not refuse our love.

However, even if you do so – we forgive you. Relax your urge to control. Trust us! Trust yourself in us!

Oliver is waking up.

OLIVER

Good morning, Tina.

TINA

Good morning. Sorry if I woke you up? I had an urge to write something and wanted to do it while the inspiration was still strong.

OLIVER

All fine. I usually wake up around this time. Any fresh news from Max?

TINA

Not yet, but I hope – soon there will be.

OLIVER

Do you mind if I head for London ASAP? I have so much to do now!

TINA

Sure, as you wish. Let's have
breakfast together first! Do you like
porridge?

50. INT. CAMBRIDGE, ERIC'S MOTHER HOUSE –
THE SAME DAY, LATE MORNING

DANIEL

Mrs Foss, the crumble was
impressive – as always. Thank you so
much for this treat.

MRS FOSS

I am glad. I am glad. Excuse me for
I will have to leave you now. Daniel,
please, send regards to your family.

DANIEL

Certainly. Have a good day, Mrs Foss.

ERIC

Bye, Mum.

Daniel's mother leaves.

DANIEL

What has brought you to Cambridge
so soon?

ERIC

As a matter of fact, I am following
a case which brought me exactly to
Cambridge.

DANIEL

How interesting!

51. EXT. / INT. CAMBRIDGE, POLICE STATION –
     THE SAME DAY, MIDDAY (CONTINUED)

Eric is entering the police building.

His mobile phone rings. A friend of his mother, Mrs BLACK, calls and speaks while still in shock:

MRS BLACK (V.O.)

Eric, your Mother, you know, we were playing cards, our usual Sunday group... she suddenly lost her mind... she cannot communicate at all.

Eric's face shows no change.

52. INT. CAMBRIDGE, POLICE STATION – THE SAME DAY, MIDDAY (CONTINUED)

Max is sitting in the interrogation room, facing the tinted glass room-partition which does not allow him to see through it.

Eric is seated in the room on the other side of that glass partition. He can see Max.

ERIC

Is it true that you are not denying your global activity in promoting ETs intervention on Earth?

MAX

Yes. It is.

ERIC

That is a problem –

Max finishes this sentence

MAX

– only to those who consider themselves the top ruling authority on the planet. Is there a law that describes my act as criminal? On which premise are you taking my freedom away and keeping me locked here?

ERIC

ETs are a very sensitive topic – hence not an usual one on our public communication platforms.

MAX

And, you are making sure it remains that way forever – even in the face of a devastating cosmic influence that is being experienced on the planet? You obviously don't have anybody in your family who has turned into a vegetative state after a sudden deterioration of their cerebral functions! Besides, have you checked with the scientific community – WHAT THEY ARE DOING TO HELP HUMANITY IN THIS PARTICULAR SITUATION? Are you

going to imprison them because they
have not found the solution yet –
even though THEY ARE PAID to direct
all their research for the wellbeing of
people and the planet?

Max takes a break as if giving a chance to Eric to speak.

Met with silence, Max continues:

MAX (CONT'D)

You were fast to capture a volunteer,
the representative of youth, who
does not think within the old
paradigm and to give him a lesson on
how dangerous it is to do anything
with ETs. I think, now, while a good
part of the global population is
turning into a sad helpless lot, it is
more dangerous to hide the truth
and be passive than work on finding
a solution. By the way, do you
personally do anything towards those
solutions? Do you really believe that
chasing sincere people, who invest
themselves in helping humanity, is
the most you can and should do in
this life on Earth that the universe
has granted to you?

*Eric does not show a single sign of authority, agreement
or disagreement.*

MAX (CONT'D)

I think all barriers we've erected to
cocoon ourselves need to fall down.
There is no difference between you
and me. If anything, this planetary

problem should teach us that! We should work together for the same goal – not against one another. Sorry Mr. Investigating Officer, for this lengthy monologue.

ERIC

I hear you. Thank you, Max Gosh.

53. INT. DANIEL'S HOUSE – THE SAME DAY, SUNDAY MIDDAY (CONTINUED)

Tina enters her family home and finds her father in the kitchen pouring water into a kettle.

TINA

Hi, Dad! Can you, please, count me in for a cup of tea?

DANIEL

Certainly – since having tea with you has become a very rare opportunity recently. I am glad you still come to this house!

TINA

I do – though not that often, as you've noticed, since we are very busy at Max's place.

Tina disappears from the kitchen.

We see Daniel preparing tea for two.

As he finishes, Tina appears. Her hands are full of various items from pieces of her clothes to cosmetics,

USB sticks, and a backpack. She is organising her backpack...

Daniel moves a cup of tea in front of Tina.

Her main focus continues to be sorting out her belongings.

TINA

Thanks Dad. It's very kind of you.

DANIEL

My pleasure.

Daniel watches Tina's busyness in silence for a while.

DANIEL (CONT'D)

Over there, at Max's, you said you are busy. Busy with what?

TINA

Gosh, Dad! Busy helping the world at this difficult time! I think everybody on the planet should find time for it – not think about themselves only. What happened to your three MBA friends? And where is Mark? Has he moved out?

DANIEL

Mark is in the States, at a gathering of scientists. My three MBA pals are fine – though their enquiry for more information about the situation with elderly people did not give any results.

TINA

I hope they've learnt to listen to
their inner voice rather than various
mediums. The age of mediums is
over.

DANIEL

But you believed in the initial
messages of those mediums – didn't
you!? Now, you relativise the validity
of their messages!?

TINA

Well noticed, Dad. Yes, I accepted
their first messages. I listened to how
my entire body responded to them.
They resonated with me. As we
see, life is now showing these were
correct messages.

DANIEL

Are you saying that any further
information from the mediums is
incorrect?

TINA

Information channelled through
mediums is not always correct – it
would be very simple if it was.

DANIEL

I am not sure I understand all that
business with the open channels.

TINA

Don't worry, Dad. Even many of
those who are open channels and
receive messages, also do not
understand it fully. There was a time
when channelled information was
a novelty – and served to speed
up the expansion of awareness.
However, time has changed. Now,
even mediums are expected to roll
up their sleeves and do concrete
work for humanity. They could get
involved in voluntary work – should
they be ready, as there is a network
of volunteers around the world.
Dad, why don't you come to Max's
place to be inspired with my friends
and, perhaps, find how you could
contribute.

DANIEL

Why not! I met Eric earlier today. He
might still be in Cambridge. Do you
mind if I invite him as well?

TINA

Of course not. So, see you later.

*Having sorted out her backpack, Tina swiftly makes
her move, kisses her dad and leaves the kitchen.*

From outside kitchen, we hear her:

TINA (O.S.)

Ahhh, Dad, how is grandpa?

DANIEL

Grandpa is still the same... no further
deterioration – no improvement.

*Tina sticks her head out from behind the kitchen door,
as if to emphasise:*

TINA

Sometimes NO CHANGE is great
news. Bye, Dad.

DANIEL

Tina, you have not finished your
tea!?

54.   INT. DANIEL'S HOUSE – THE SAME DAY,
      SUNDAY EVENING (CONTINUED)

*With a cup of tea in his hand, Daniel moves to the
lounge and sits comfortably in his favourite armchair.*

In that instant his mobile phone rings.

ERIC

Hi, Dan. Sorry for disturbing you on
this Sunday afternoon, but I have
terrible news. After my mother left us
to play cards with her friends, I was
informed that she suddenly lost her
capacity to think and express herself
in a meaningful way. I am going to
see her now.

DANIEL

Oh, Eric! I'll come and join you.

55. INT. MAX'S FLAT – THE SAME DAY, SUNDAY EVENING

The usual crowd (Max, Tina, Maggy, Kate, Josh, Ann) are in the living area.

Some are gathered by the computer, others discuss things while scattered on the sofa, armchairs and the floor.

Daniel and Eric are being ushered in by Tina.

TINA

As I've mentioned, I invited my Dad to get informed about our activities and he invited his friend Eric. So here they are.

Tina then introduces her friends to her two guests.

TINA (CONT'D)

This is Josh, Maggy, Ann, Kate and my boyfriend Max – Max Gosh. Eric, you might already be familiar with that name since it has been flooding social media for the last 24 hours.

Eric shows no signs of reaction to this remark.

DANIEL

Hi guys. We are here to learn from you. Eric's mother has just been affected with the cosmic energy, or whatever that is. We visited her in hospital.

MAX

(to Eric)

Sorry to hear that.

ERIC

Life can surprise us in many ways.
Without warning, it can signal a
necessity to change ourselves.
Kids, I am eager to hear about your
activities and see whether I could
fit somewhere to complement your
efforts.

TINA

You, and your friends, your
generation, could organize into, for
example, an international PARENTS
group. You could develop help-
centres of various kinds: counselling
and financial support... or, once you
put yourself into it, you will have a
good picture on what else is needed
and what the priorities are.

ANN

Besides your personal network of
friends that you might contact, what
we could do is ask our generation for
the contact details of their parents
and with their permission pass it to
you. You will soon have so much on
your plate.

56. INT. MAX'S FLAT – THE SAME DAY, SUNDAY EVENING (CONTINUED)

We see Tina, Ann, Kate and Daniel gathered in front of Max's computer, where Tina is showing to others something on the computer screen.

The rest of the crowd is on other side of the living room. We follow their conversation.

ERIC

Do we have to work in groups of 3, as you do?

JOSH

Not necessarily. Yet, since numbers are behind everything – it is good to use them consciously.

MAGGY

We believe that 3 stands for the primary value of UNITY. As all our activities are focused on building unity, we base them on that number.

MAX

If all of us work for the same purpose, to me, it makes sense that we use the same operational system. However, it is truly up to you, PARENTS.

DANIEL

(addresses all)

Thanks for inviting us into the global action network. We are impressed and it will be our honour to support you. Eric and I will leave now.

57.   INT. MAX'S FLAT – THE SAME DAY, SUNDAY EVENING (CONTINUED)

Max is escorting Daniel and Eric to the flat's entrance door.

They all stop at the entrance hall.

MAX

Eric, sorry, but your voice sounds familiar to me. Have we met before?

ERIC

As a matter of fact – yes. We communicated a few hours ago, with a tinted glass partition between us.

MAX

Don't tell me that it was you on the other side! What brought you here? The episode with your mother?

ERIC

Not really. Your words brought me here. My Mother's episode has just given me even more motivation to care. I was thinking if I ever find you, to thank you in person for being who you are.

58.   INT. USA, SCIENTISTS' MEETING – DAY

A big conference room accommodates a group of nearly 150 scientists gathered to discuss Cloud-X.

Each has their country name and their personal name in front of them.

A huge screen features those who speak.

MR PREBOY – USA

Perhaps, we could shield the entire planet with a blanket that will be impenetrable to dangerous frequencies?

MR KOVALENKO – RUSSIA

I see, it sounds like an automatic defence idea. However, there are some problems there.

First, do you think with our technology we are able to control the power of celestial influences as vast as this interstellar cloud? Also, if we even manage to design and activate a shield, it might stop some natural influences that are vital for all life on the planet. In other words, we could stop one problem and invite another.

MR GREEN – UK

What are you saying then? Are you suggesting a surrender?

MR KOVALENKO – RUSSIA

No, I am not advocating a surrender, but a need for a completely new approach.

MR TURMEL – FRANCE

Such as?

MR KOVALENKO – RUSSIA

I do not know yet, but I believe it is not out of reach – otherwise we would not have found ourselves in this whole scenario.

MR GAMBARA – ITALY

Do you also have any idea where to look for a better approach?

MR KOVALENKO – RUSSIA

Not at the moment, yet I am not assuming myself powerless and incapable of finding the answer. One thing I know is that we should all look very deep inside our own self, even when faced with a planetary problem. I believe that when we reach our essence-self, in that boundless ONENESS, the questions and answers are all there together.

MR TAYLOR – UK

Mr. Kovalenko, I can only say that you are floating above the material ground. Besides, I did not think we are gathered here to produce a spiritual overview of the current situation and to figure out guidance from that perspective.

MR ADAMS – USA

I agree, Mr Kovalenko, your approach is yours – that is fine. However, may I remind you that this is the meeting of scientific minds. However, you seem to be suggesting that not only scientists but spiritual people are to have a go in finding a feasible solution for this situation!?

MR KOVALENKO – RUSSIA

Mr Adams, it is not about competition. All I am trying to say is that a new paradigm needs to be reached to tackle this enormous planetary challenge – the biggest of all I've known of. That new paradigm requires thinking out of the box and accepting everybody's viewpoint.

MARK

Our competitive and ego-driven approach will never save the planet. If anything, with such a level of consciousness we will definitely be doomed to perish. The challenge we are facing requires the use of the entire human potential – not just scientific minds.

MR SMITH – UK

Mr Kovalenko, I might be wrong, but I am under the impression that you expect all of us to follow your logic and understanding of the given circumstances. That, of course, is impossible.

MR KOVALENKO – RUSSIA

Sorry for being misunderstood. I believe we need to agree as a collective – whosoever idea or solution we think is the best. I did not assume it is mine – though I suggested a way forward.

MR PATEL – INDIA

Lifeforms exist in relation to the energy of their environment. They survive and progress according to their ability to adapt, therefore upgrade. A major job of such a kind is upon humanity now. We could say – suddenly, but I doubt that it is outside the celestial schedule for this planet and its current population.

Many turn their heads to Mr Patel.

MR SHOLTZ – GERMANY

How can we then adapt NOW, Mr Patel?

MR PATEL – INDIA

That is exactly what spiritual literature and sacred teachings and practices are focused on. As you asked me, my answer is:

BY CONSCIOUSLY STRIVING TO BECOME EVEN BETTER – both as individuals and society.

MR ED MORISON – UK

You are sounding as if revealing something epochal, but all you are doing is re-inventing the wheel.

MR PATEL – INDIA

You may see it that way, but faced with a possible global collapse, what is more important than to be humane: kind and supportive. If we express care and love at each moment, it will soothe the roughness of the experience. My suggestion is: let's UNITE! Let us get together globally and establish a Planetary Scientific Community to address the burning planetary issues in a constructive way that will save all humanity ASAP.

MR ED MORISON – UK

Gosh, you spiritually minded people cannot leave others alone to their own knowledge and guidance, but persistently serve your narrative about unity. Are we not already united here, at this conference?

MR PATEL – INDIA

If we had really been pushing our narrative, maybe the world would have become a much better place. But spirituality is not about pushing and imposing. I agree – having met for a conference like this one is a big achievement, but the unity I am talking about assumes an uncompromising drive from the inner self to improve, grow, help and support one another and all humanity and all the time.

MR MARK BARRETT

I would add that humanity cannot make significant progress until scientific and spiritual communities understand that they are on the same quest – and hence join forces. Projected on an individual, it means that the heart and mind should be in balance. So, there are many aspects and stages of unity.

MR ED MORISON – UK

That stereotypical narrative, I want to say, what did you say... sorry... what...

Ed's entire body language starts to change, particularly his facial expression – all indicating a great effort in dealing with thoughts, memory, and capacity to speak. Eventually, he loses them all.

Long silence, loaded with shock and unease of all witnesses.

Mark and Mr Patel run to help Ed.

> MR PATEL – INDIA
>
> Are you ok? Relax. Relax.

59. EXT. CAMBRIDGE, STREET OUTSIDE DANIEL'S HOUSE – NIGHT

Daniel parks his car and steps out.

At that instant a taxi stops next to him.

Mark is exiting taxi.

> DANIEL
>
> Look who is here! Welcome from the US!

> MARK
>
> I am glad I am back.

They hug and move towards the entrance to Daniel's house.

60. INT. DANIEL'S HOUSE, LOUNGE – NIGHT (CONTINUED)

Daniel and Mark are still standing in the living room.

> DANIEL
>
> So, how was the conference?

> MARK
>
> I don't know what to say and not to sound disappointed. Ok. The positive

thing is I did meet some remarkable professionals, expanded my social network – and that's about it.

DANIEL

How about a common ground for a global action! Did you discuss it?

MARK

I am disillusioned about uniting scientists worldwide. Their research and focus seem to be driven by so many different motives. Even in the difficult global situation as it is now, I would say conscience is leading only a minority of them.

DANIEL

You could perhaps work with those who follow the voice of their conscience?

MARK

Yes, I could and I will. But my expectations were bigger.

DANIEL

Unfortunately, expectations easily lead to disappointment.

MARK

I can see that.

DANIEL

Mark, you have already done a lot regarding Cloud-X's influence on

Earth – you have spread the word about it in your TV interview, which has started a great motion. Yes, we can always do more – some people wish that all the time. I understand you.

MARK

I suppose so.

DANIEL

Me and Eric have just decided to work on, what my Tina named, "Parents for Humanity" Group. You could be the third member in our group.

Mark thinks for a while.

MARK

It seems natural to accept your offer even though I am not a father. It will ground me. Hopefully, I will bring some scientist into that network – and add an astrophysics' note to it!

Mark finally changes his facial expression, by showing a modest smile.

DANIEL

Great! You will link our generation to the sky.

61. INT. SPACESHIP MANNA-373 – DAY

Faro and Ita are seated at their adjacent working locations.

We see Faro choosing PLANETARY UPDATES – Milky Way, Solar System 1, planet Earth.

The left half of the space above the desk becomes a cosmic environment showing a 3D planet Earth scaled to fit to available space.

Triangles in green, purple, and brown, are scattered across the planetary globe.

> ITA

What are those triangles?

> FARO

In their humanitarian efforts, the humans on Earth have started to organise themselves in groups of 3, which are shown as triangles. Green triangles stand for youth's asking us to help their planet; Purple triangles represent the young individuals engaged in some form of care about affected people; and Brown triangles represent the Parents Groups activities.

> ITA

And the red dots?

> FARO

Those stand for people negatively affected with the cosmic influence – the older individuals.

The right half of the space above the desk becomes an excel-type table floating in the air.

Each of the first three rows are dedicated to one of three major actions of the population on Earth (Green, Purple and Brown – as described above).

Columns stand for the number of days counted from the day Cloud-X was announced to Earth via three individuals. These columns are named by numbers of the Fibonacci series: starting from 3, then, 5, 8, 13, 21, 34, 55, 89, 144, 233, and so on.

The columns up to the one titled 34 are all filled in with numbers.

The fourth row shows the sum of the figures in the column above.

We follow the increasing vale of numbers regarding all the motions shown on the table.

ITA

For how long will we monitor these groups?

FARO

We will monitor them until the critical point is reached – in whatever direction.

ITA

There is another table! What is that one for?

FARO

It shows the number of people on Earth, the number of old people (over 65), the number of adults (age 35-60), the number of young people (age 18-35), and the number of the affected individuals (red dots on the globe). By the way, at the moment, 55% of old people are affected.

62.   INT. SPACECRAFT MANNA-373 – DAY

Faro and Ita are monitoring the situation on Earth, on the 144th day.

We see the familiar Earth's excel table as a stream of data floating above Faro's desk.

This time, we also see columns 55 and 89 filled in with data.

As Faro and Ita are watching, the numbers in column 144 are changing, growing in value – as the data is being received and updated.

At one moment, updating stops, highlighting column 144 with a twinkling light and a beeping sound.

The average of the three numbers, at the bottom row of each column (144th-day column), shows 61.8.

ITA

What is that?

FARO

The indication of the critical point being reached: 39.2% to 61.8% – 61.8% being the population united in spontaneous effort to help.

ITA

The Golden Number PHI, (1.618 or,
equally 0.618)! AGAIN! Now I see
why you seem to be obsessed with it.

FARO

If the Creator was obsessed with it,
why could I not be?

ITA

What fascinates you there?

FARO

First, it is a NUMBER (1.618.......) that
connects two relationships into a
perfect proportionality. Secondly, Phi
is the key to perpetual harmony and
beauty. Thirdly, it provides infinite
sustainability.

ITA

Faro, what is actually new to finding
numbers behind everything?

A long thoughtful pause from Faro.

*He switches to a different display that illustrates the
presence of PHI in nature's design.*

*We see spiral galaxies, a nautilus shell, fruits,
vegetables, a pentagon with diagonals, flowers, a
human body, etc.*

FARO

Yes, it is not a surprise that numbers
are employed throughout creation.
What's fascinating is that the design

properties of seemingly endless shapes, processes, growth, etc., are provided by a single number – as a value of one proportion, the Golden Proportion! Just look and admire.

ITA

Woow! Where are those images collected?

FARO

Elsewhere, in natural worlds!

ITA

What a mastery of the Designer!

63. PLANET EARTH GLOBALLY – 144TH DAY IN COSMIC CHART

Sky speaks and holographic images are projected.

Global overview of the planet.

Usual movements and activities go on.

At the same moment, all phones on the planet start ringing in a cacophony of different tunes.

People are picking up their mobile phones and soon hear an alien voice, addressing all of humanity.

We hear the voice delivering the same messages in all languages across the planet.

Sound travels through the air across the globe, and merges into an awesome reverberating recitation that penetrates to the bones.

VOICE OF THE SKY (V.O.)

AVE, INMORTALES, AVE...

We have been waiting for your unity
driven by higher causes.

We are happy to see you acting
globally on a single issue while
maintaining composure in the most
challenging times. It has been our
dream to meet you at such a level of
consciousness.

We congratulate you and respect
you. Love to you all – until we meet
at even higher coordinates.

*Disbelief, confusion, shock, joy – all kinds of feelings
are popping up in response to what is being witnessed.*

*As the mysterious message ends, an equally mysterious
colour- performance floods the sky.*

64.   EXT. CAMBRIDGE, OUTSIDE AN ELDERLY
      HOME – NEXT DAY, MIDDAY

*A sunny day, the 145th in the celestial chart created in
regards to Cloud-X.*

*Eric is in his car, on the way to the elderly home where
his mother is accommodated.*

65.   INT. CAMBRIDGE, ELDERLY HOME – MIDDAY

A nurse is escorting Eric to his mother's room.

NURSE

Thank you for coming to see your
mother. Be prepared for a surprise.

ERIC

If it is a good one, it is more than
welcome.

The nurse escorts Eric to the room where his mother is.

The door of the room is open.

*Taken by a surprising scene inside the room, Eric stops
at the door.*

*His mother is chatting with MARGARET – the lady she
shares the room with.*

*Both of them are sitting on their beds, fully dressed
and engaged in a joyful conversation.*

ERIC'S MOTHER

All Italian cities are like a history
of art under the open sky, isn't it
Margaret?

I love Siena, particularly horse racing
on that magnificent piazza –

MARGARET

– and the beautiful white medieval
buildings –

ERIC'S MOTHER

– you feel as if at any moment a fully
armed knight on his horse will appear
from behind the next corner.

ERIC

Good morning, ladies.

The old ladies turn towards the room's entrance where the statement is coming from and see Eric.

ERIC'S MOTHER

You are already here. Great. The nurse told me you'll come today. I am ready. Margaret, is anybody going to pick you up? Do you want us to give you a lift?

We hear the voice of the nurse, who enters the room after Eric.

NURSE

Margaret, you daughter will be here soon.

The nurse leaves the room.

Eric remains there. His capacity to hide his feelings is efficient as always. However, what is going on around him is under his serious scrutiny.

ERIC'S INNER VOICE (V.O.)

How? When? Who?

Resisting this cacophony, Eric steps towards his mother to embrace her.

Before Eric reaches her bed, his mother literally jumps up and rushes to hug him.

ERIC'S MOTHER

So nice of you to come today.

66.   INT. / EXT. ERIC'S CAR – DAY

Eric is driving his mother back to her home.

ERIC'S MOTHER

Why was I in the elderly home?

ERIC

It seemed proper at the time. Now,
you are returning home.

ERIC'S MOTHER

God is so merciful! Have I not been
telling you that all the time?

ERIC

Indeed, HE IS.

Eric, switches on the car radio. Music; then news time.

RADIO SPEAKER (V.O.)

This morning the reports across
the world are confirming that
elderly people, who have recently
experienced problems with memory,
are returned not only to their
cerebral capacity prior to falling into
that condition, but seemingly fresher
and extremely enthusiastic about life.
More on this in our evening news.

ERIC'S MOTHER

What cases are they talking about?

ERIC

Something about the past. But it
does not matter anymore.

ERIC'S MOTHER

You are right. What matters is NOW.
This moment! Every moment to live!
What a blessing.

ERIC

Mom, I am so grateful for accepting
me to be your child. I can never
thank you enough for that.

67.   INT. OXFORD, MARK'S HOUSE – SAME DAY
      (CONTINUED)

Mark is unlocking his home with flowers in his hand.

*Zoe notices motion in the main entrance, and heads in
that direction.*

The door opens and Mark steps in.

*Excited to see Mark, Zoe rushes towards him and hangs
herself around his neck...*

ZOE

Darling, you are back! What a day!
Dad also phoned me saying mother
is perfectly fine again. What is going
on?

They kiss.

Eric hands the flowers to her.

They move to the kitchen where Zoe is sorting out flowers.

MARK

What is going on? We might never know what is really going on with the world or else. But whoever/whatever navigates the processes, I salute that power. To learn to cooperate with it, would be worth any troubles.

ZOE

But, perhaps, first, we should learn to cooperate with one another.

MARK

I suppose so.

ZOE

May I start with a big apology to you?

MARK

For what?

ZOE

I was so shortsighted when I asked you to leave, so focused on myself.

MARK

I could say the same – I was focused on my single goal at that moment which was to help humanity.

A short silence – though not unpleasant.

MARK (CONT'D)

That is still my aim.

ZOE

Now I understand but do not object.
You may ask WHY and HOW come.

MARK

But I do not need to. We've learnt a
lot recently. Have we not?

*By this time, Zoe has placed the flowers in a vase and
moves to kiss Mark.*

Tenderness and love fill the space.

68.   INT. SPACECRAFT MANA-373 – DAY

CAPTAIN URROS

Yes, we helped them, yet on their
current level of consciousness they
are not allowed to know how we
did it. After seeing the result of
our global overnight intervention,
they will be puzzled as to what and
how the change took place. Some
will conclude that their joint action
driven by essence desire, their
meditations, visualizations, and the
trust in us, worked. And that is fine.
But, most of all, what they need to
be aware of is the power of their
intent and unity.

FARO

On what premise have we helped
them?

CAPTAIN URROS

Their youth loved and cared for
their elders, sacrificed themselves,
then organised globally for the
common good of all humanity. By
doing so, they raised the vibrational
level on the planet and so created
a new energy template on it. Their
scientists united in a number, as
never before – though remained
insufficiently productive. On the
other hand, spiritually minded
individuals massively focused on a
positive outcome ... Upon the overall
results achieved within the time
frame given to the Earth's population
and the level of unity demonstrated,
we just had to act as the Universal
Laws command. So, we did. We
provided new entities to inhabit the
bodies of those aged 50+ who could
not cope with energy on the planet.
The evacuated entities were thus
released to go to dimensions better
suitable to their evolution.

FARO

It says to me that... No energy in
existence is ever wasted.

CAPTAIN URROS

All energies are brought into
being for a particular purpose and
therefore are equally precious. We
do not punish them, just facilitate
their evolution the best we can.

ITA

What about Cloud-X?

CAPTAIN URROS

The energy of Cloud-X helped in
the selection process. Those who
self-selected, as incompatible with
the strong Cloud-X energy, were
replaced. That way, the whole planet
was reinforced to a level where
higher human potentials can be lived.

ITA

Does it mean that Cloud-X saved the
planet?

CAPTAIN URROS

Cloud-X was a transition stage – a
preparation for a new reality of
perfect human beings. If nobody
could receive its energy, all of Earth's
population would be effaced by the
next natural cosmic ripple that is on
its way to them. Upgrading through
stronger energy is an imperative in
order to continue existing.

*While captain Urros is talking, we see a collage of
scenes across the planet:*

- *Elderly people with their family members on family lunches, then working as professionals in various business settings, also walking through fields, biking, playing games – all energetic and full of joy.*
- *Daniel's parents are visiting Daniel. Three generations are playing board games and all are equally invested in fun and laughter. Daniel's mobile phone rings: Bruno and Chen are calling. We do not hear their conversations, but see their excited faces and the atmosphere in their countries.*
- *Brazil is flooded by carnival-type outdoor celebrations; Africa and China are also in a festive mood. We witness the global proportions of relief and happiness.*

69. INT. COMPUTER SCREENS ACROSS THE GLOBE

Youth activists from the global salvation network are sitting in front of their computer screens.

At the beginning, we see their screens only, featuring a cosmic background and the stream of flowing sentences:

- *AVE IMMORTALS, AVE*
- *Thank you, cosmic family.*
- *Love – Self-sacrifice – Unity is your and our common world*
- *We are your humble siblings.*

Then, an interference on all their screens across the globe.

A Celestial transmission cuts in:

- *"We see you clearly and are proud of your maturity.*
- *You are able to create a perfect world on Earth, and provide its shift into a galactic community of advanced civilisations.*
- *As your elder brothers and sisters, we await that moment most eagerly.*
- *AVE IMMORTALS, AVE"*

70. INT. OXFORD, MAX'S FLAT – DAY

Zooming out from the computer screens in the previous scene, shows Tina, Maggy, Kate, Josh, Ann, Oliver and Max, watching the ETs addressing them.

Deep calm is flooding the space.

The celestial transmission ends.

After a good while...

OLIVER

Interesting – isn't it: ET's use the same greetings as we do: "AVE IMMORTALS, AVE"

MAX

Our Dimensions are obviously connected. Not only that: there is an intentional mental communication between them.

TINA

Wait a second! How can we know that our thoughts and ideas are really ours? Where do they really originate from?

OLIVER

And inspiration?

MAX

Obviously, we cannot know that — the same way that parents cannot tell their kids everything parents know.

MAGGI

Don't you think that our thoughts are known to celestial friends?

MAX

I need not to think it — I know they do.

KATE

Can they influence us?

OLIVER

The influence I am receiving now says: Let's celebrate!

MAX

Absolutely!

In no time Max switches on music, gets the Champagne and glasses out, Tina brings snacks.

The party unfolds with Queen's song "We are the Champions".

71.   EXT. GLOBAL SCENES

Zoom across the planet to show the global celebration.

Waves of excitement are traveling through continents.

Amongst the dancing bodies on the streets:

- *in Rio – we see Bruno;*
- *in China – we see Chen;*
- *in Africa – we see Aabi;*
- *on the streets of London – we see Liam and Nora dancing together with a happy crowd;*
- *in Cambridge – Eric, his Mom and Dainel with his family are amongst elated people;*
- *in Oxford – Mark and Zoe are experiencing the same.*

It is the body language of joy beyond words that expresses the magnitude of this moment.

72. EXT. CAM RIVER, CAMBRIDGE

Max and Tina are sitting on a boat floating in the river Cam.

They are facing the same direction; he hugs her torso from the back.

The magic of a deep and mutual contentment is in the air.

After a long while...

TINA

Any fresh conclusion on testing
the power of love? Has love been
delivering according to your
understanding of it?

MAX

Oh yes, and more so. It showed me the power of UNITY.

THE END

Published by
MILENA
milena@milena.org.uk

Printed by
Lightning Source, UK

A catalogue record for this book is available from the British Library

ISBN
978-1-909323-22-3